THE MARK OF THE CROWN

JEDI APPRENTICE

The Mark of the Crown

Jude Watson

SCHOLASTIC INC.

New York Toronto London Auckland Sydney
Mexico City New Delhi Hong Kong

Cover design by Madalina Stefan. Cover art by Cliff Nielsen.

Scholastic Children's Books
Commonwealth House, 1-19 New Oxford Street, London WC1A 1NU
a division of Scholastic Ltd
London — New York — Toronto — Sydney — Auckland
Mexico City — New Delhi — Hong Kong

Published in the UK by Scholastic Ltd, 2000
Published in the USA by Scholastic Inc., 1999

ISBN 0 439 01448 4

1 3 5 7 9 10 8 6 4 2

Printed in the U.S.A.

THE MARK OF THE CROWN

As soon as Obi-Wan Kenobi and Qui-Gon Jinn stepped off the departure ramp of their transport onto the planet of Gala, a cloud car purred to a stop at their feet.

The door opened noiselessly. A ramp slid down. A driver dressed in a navy tunic and pants scrambled out, then waited by the open door. Inside, Obi-Wan glimpsed a luxurious interior.

"Queen Veda has sent her personal transport for the Jedi," the driver announced.

"Please thank the Queen for her hospitality," Qui-Gon said with a small bow. "It is such a fine day. We prefer to walk to the palace."

The driver looked startled. "But the Queen instructed me to —"

"Thank you," Qui-Gon said firmly, and walked past the driver.

Obi-Wan followed his Master. He knew that

the weather had nothing to do with why Qui-Gon had decided to walk. A Jedi mission began the moment a Jedi's feet touched the surface of a new planet. Every sense he or she had was to be focused on the surroundings. Attunement to sight, smell, sound, and touch helped to bring the Force to bear. It was said that some Jedi Masters could see all the way to the end of a mission just by taking a few short steps on a new world.

Thirteen-year-old Obi-Wan wasn't a Master — or even a Jedi Knight — yet. As an apprentice, he had a long journey ahead. But even an apprentice could feel the dark tremors rippling under the calm surface of Galu, the capital city of Gala. Obi-Wan couldn't see to the end of the mission, but he could already sense that success would be hard-won, and far from assured.

They exited the spaceport and entered the wide boulevards of the city. Galu was a city built on three hills. On top of the tallest hill was the gleaming white palace, visible from any point on the city streets.

Gala had once been a prosperous planet, the jewel of its system. It still had its share of rich citizens, but the gap between those with wealth and those without was wide. Even as cloud cars almost as luxurious as the Queen's hummed by, beggars groveled for credits and food on the city streets.

Obi-Wan had been to Galu on his last mission. He had already seen the decay behind the once-grand buildings. The stone was chipped and weathered, and had not been restored. Graceful lindemor trees had once bloomed along the wide boulevards, but now they stood abandoned, dead, and twisted, rising up from the ground like clawing fingers.

"The Queen has made the right decision," Qui-Gon remarked. "Elections should stabilize the planet. It is time for democracy to come to Gala."

"Past time, it seems to me," Obi-Wan agreed. "Why do you think Queen Veda made the decision now?"

"There was great danger of a civil war here," Qui-Gon said. "The Tallah dynasty has ruled for a thousand years. They were successful at one time. But power can corrupt. After King Cana died, the Queen knew that the power of the monarchy was slipping. She gave in to the people's wishes and opened the government to elections."

"Which is why her son, Prince Beju, may be dangerous," Obi-Wan said. "How do you think the Prince will react when he sees us?"

Just days ago, the Jedi had thwarted the Prince's scheme to become a hero to the Galacian people. Prince Beju had caused a bacta shortage on Gala. Bacta was a substance used to heal wounds and regenerate damaged flesh. Its miraculous properties saved lives. After he'd created the fake shortage, the Prince had made an agreement with the Syndicat, an illegal political group on neighboring Phindar, to bring some of their bacta home with him. Obi-Wan had foiled the plan by posing as the Prince and helping Phindar's citizens remove the Syndicat from power.

"I don't think he'll greet me with open arms," Obi-Wan continued. "After all, I *did* kidnap him."

"He has much to lose if he opposes us," Qui-Gon pointed out. "He might have had help with that bacta scheme, but I'm fairly certain it wasn't from Queen Veda. If we keep silent about what we know happened on Phindar, no doubt the Prince will as well."

"Good," Obi-Wan said.

"But he will still see us as the enemy," Qui-Gon added.

Inwardly, Obi-Wan gave a sigh. Qui-Gon often told him reassuring news, only to contradict it in the next sentence. It was his way of telling Obi-Wan that situations were not fixed, but fluid. "Count on nothing. Only change," Qui-Gon had told him several times. He was always right.

Suddenly, Obi-Wan felt a disturbance in the Force like a dark wave.

"Yes," Qui-Gon murmured.

They stopped for a moment. The street they had turned down was deserted. And then they heard the sound of shouting.

They moved together, without speaking, toward the sound. Neither one reached for his lightsaber, or even rested a hand on the hilt. But every nerve was poised, on alert.

Suddenly, a crowd surged around a corner, heading for them. They carried laser-pulsating signs that spelled out DECA.

Obi-Wan relaxed. It was a political rally, he realized. Deca Brun was one of the candidates for Governor of Gala.

"Already democracy is working," he observed. The people cheered as the laser sign flashed gold, then blue.

Qui-Gon was still alert. "Something else," he murmured. He turned to look back.

From an intersecting narrow street behind them, another crowd suddenly spilled onto the boulevard. They bore signs reading WILA PRAMMI.

"Wila Prammi, the third candidate," Obi-Wan

noted. Yoda had briefed the Jedi on the two candidates opposing Prince Beju.

The Deca Brun crowd surged forward, and the Prammi supporters ran to meet them. Obi-Wan and Qui-Gon were caught in the middle. All of a sudden, signs were used as clubs, and fists and feet flew as the two groups attacked each other.

Obi-Wan looked at Qui-Gon. This was not a time for lightsabers. Neither of the two groups had blast weapons. But still, the Jedi were in danger. They were in the middle of a brawling mob.

A burly Galacian man holding a laser sign suddenly lunged at Obi-Wan, his sign held high. Leading with his left shoulder, Obi-Wan went into a roll. He sprang to his feet only meters away as the sign glanced off someone else's shoulder.

Two Deca supporters held Qui-Gon's arms as a third pulled a fist back to strike him. Qui-Gon employed a classic Jedi escape technique, twisting his body and striking upward with his head. The two Deca supporters were left with sore arms and ringing ears. They looked around for Qui-Gon, but he was already gone, heading for Obi-Wan at the sidelines.

"We can't do anything here," he told Obi-Wan. "Let's keep moving."

They dodged a Wila Prammi supporter as she tripped a Deca supporter, then smashed him on the head. "The road to democracy can be a rough one," Qui-Gon observed as they hurried past. "But on Gala, it seems rougher than most."

The Grand Palace of Gala rose before them, an impressive, sprawling white building with two tall towers. Surrounding the windows and inlaid in the tower spires were sparkling blue azurite crystals and gems in mosaic patterns. The roof was gilded.

Together the gold roof and glittering mosaics made the palace shimmer, as if it weren't quite real.

The Jedi were led through vast hallways to the receiving room, where Queen Veda waited. She was dressed in a gown of shimmersilk that appeared to change color when she moved. Different shades of blue and green were sewn in fluttering panels that appeared and disappeared as she walked forward to greet them. Her gold headdress was studded with blue and green crystals.

Qui-Gon barely made note of her elegant

dress. He was shocked to feel her living Force. Or rather to *not* feel it. It was so dim. The Queen was only in middle age, yet he sensed a serious disturbance, as if she were extremely ill, or dying.

Qui-Gon and Obi-Wan bowed their greeting.

"I welcome the Jedi to Gala," the Queen said. Her voice still rang with firm authority. Qui-Gon wondered if she had gathered her strength for the meeting, wanting to appear well. Galacians were known for their distinctive pale skin, a bluish tone they called "moonlight." But the Queen's skin was not luminous, but an unhealthy-looking color reminiscent of bone.

"We have brought a shipment of bacta as a gift," Qui-Gon told her. "We left it at the spaceport loading dock."

"It is desperately needed here," the Queen answered. "Thank you. I'll arrange to have it distributed to the med centers."

Qui-Gon watched her face carefully. He read only relief and gratitude in her pale blue eyes, the color of ice shadows. She gave no indication that she'd heard even a whisper about Prince Beju's plan.

Still puzzled about her health, Qui-Gon studied her the way a Jedi studies, without seeming to stare. He was surprised when she boldly captured his gaze, her sharp eyes knowing.

"Yes," she said softly. "You are right. I am dying."

Qui-Gon felt Obi-Wan's start of surprise next to him. He knew the boy had not noticed the Queen's illness. Obi-Wan had excellent instincts, but often he lacked a connection to the living Force.

"My condition simplifies meetings such as this," Queen Veda continued, waving a jeweled hand. "I can be direct, and I hope you will be the same."

"We are always direct," Qui-Gon answered.

Queen Veda nodded. She lowered herself into a gilded chair and gestured for the Jedi to do so as well.

"I have thought a great deal about what I wish to leave behind," she began. "Gala needs to be a democracy. The people have asked for it, and I have granted it as my last act as Queen. That will be my legacy. There is great unrest here in the city, and in the countryside. My husband, King Cana, ruled for thirty years. His intentions were good, but corruption invaded our council of ministers and the governors of the surrounding provinces. A handful of powerful families controlled the high posts. My husband was not able to stop it. Now I am afraid of civil war. The only thing that can prevent it will be free elections. So you see why I have asked for Jedi monitoring."

Qui-Gon nodded. "What do you foresee as problems we might encounter?" he asked carefully. He didn't want to bring up Prince Beju. He wanted the Queen to introduce the topic. That would tell him where her sympathies resided.

"My son, Beju," she said flatly. "The last in line of the great Tallah dynasty — a fact he does not let you forget for a moment. All his life he has waited to rule Gala. He has not forgiven me for calling elections. He will be some trouble for you, I'm afraid. If he wins the election, he will retain the monarchy." She shrugged. "He has some support. But what he cannot inspire, he will buy or steal, I'm afraid."

Qui-Gon nodded, trying not to show his surprise at the mother's harsh words about her son.

"I will not oppose my son," Queen Veda continued. "It is true that I've denied him his birthright. I owe him my loyalty at least. I won't endorse another candidate publicly. But privately, I wish my son to lose. It is not only best for Gala. It is best for Beju. I wish him to become a private citizen, to be rid of all this." She waved her hand to take in the immense chamber. "I saw what this power did to my husband.

It corrupted him, and he was a good man. I do not want to see my son suffer the same fate. He's only sixteen. He will understand in time why I've done this. *He* is also my legacy," Queen Veda finished softly. "I wish to leave behind a son with a life that is good."

"Do you think he has a chance to win?" Qui-Gon asked.

The Queen frowned. "There is still a core of royalist supporters. The Prince has been secluded for much of his life, since we feared for his safety. He was even schooled off-planet. Not much is known about him, and that can work in his favor. He might be able to squeak by. I do hope not."

Queen Veda smiled at Qui-Gon. "You are surprised at my honesty. When time runs out, you don't waste it by fooling yourself."

"What about the other candidates, Deca Brun and Wila Prammi?" Obi-Wan asked. "Is there a favorite?"

"Deca Brun is favored," Queen Veda answered. "He's a hero to the Galacian people. He promises them reform and prosperity. It won't be that easy, but he makes it sound so."

"And Wila Prammi?" Qui-Gon prompted.

"She has more experience," the Queen replied. "She was an underminister here at the palace. Her ideas are sound and grounded in reality. Unfortunately, her palace experience hurts her in some quarters, and her bluntness hurts her in others. She has her faction, but is expected to lose."

"Were you anticipating violence?" Qui-Gon asked. "We ran into some supporters on the street. Tempers are running high."

"Yes, there have been clashes," the Queen admitted. "But I believe the people want a peaceful transition. As long as they feel the elections are honest, they won't revolt, I hope."

Queen Veda sat silently for a moment. Qui-Gon wondered if she was fading. Then he realized that she was gathering herself to say something. He knew that what she would tell them next was the real reason she had summoned them here. He glanced at Obi-Wan to make sure the boy would wait for the Queen to speak. Obi-Wan nodded.

"There is a wild card," the Queen said at last. "Another factor that is important for you to understand. Elan."

"Elan?" Qui-Gon had not heard this name before.

"There is a faction of Galacians known as the hill people," Queen Veda explained. She smoothed the tiled mosaic of the table in front of her and a piece of blue azurite came off in her hand. She rolled it in her palm, her rings flashing in the sunlight that poured through the window behind her. "Elan is their leader. The hill people are exiles who opposed the monarchy and gathered in the rough mountain terrain outside the capital city to live outside its laws. They recognize no king or queen. They are rumored to be ferocious, unfriendly. They never stay in one place for long. They raise their own food and have their own healers. They are rarely seen by outsiders. Yet they are greatly feared and hated. Elan herself is a legend, almost a ghost. I have not managed to find one person who has actually seen her."

"Will they vote in the election?" Qui-Gon asked.

Queen Veda shook her head. "No. They have refused. They were courted by both Deca Brun and Wila Prammi, but Elan refused to meet with them. She will not recognize the new governor, just as she never recognized King Cana or myself."

"If this is true, why do you call Elan a factor in the election?" Qui-Gon asked.

"Ah," the Queen said. "The last piece slips into place." She slid the piece of azurite back in the mosaic design. "Now the picture is complete."

Obi-Wan shot Qui-Gon an impatient look. Queen Veda stared down at the mosaic, lost in thought. She had gone back to the past, Qui-Gon realized.

Long moments passed before she raised her head again. "I admire your patience, Qui-Gon Jinn," she said quietly. "I wish I had that gift."

"It is not a gift, but a lesson to be relearned daily," Qui-Gon responded with a smile.

She smiled back at him, nodding slightly. "Yes, I am learning that. Which brings me to my story. When my husband, King Cana, was young, he fell in love. Our marriage had been arranged, you see. I lived in another city. We had never met. King Cana broke his vow to me and secretly married another woman. She was one of the hill people. Naturally, the Council of Ministers was outraged. They had already arranged our marriage. And the fact that King Cana had married a hill person was unacceptable. The Ministers' influence was great. They forced him to relinquish the woman. When he told his wife that he had decided to obey them, she left the city and returned to her people. He did not know it, but she was with child."

The Queen smoothed the mosaic with a hand that shook slightly. "King Cana later discovered this. Still he did not search for her. I knew nothing of this at the time. I arrived for my wedding and was married. If there was a shadow on my husband's heart, I never understood why it was there. Until the last year of his life. He told me the story. It was his greatest regret, he said. He had never recovered from the loss of his true love, or his cowardice in not seeking out his child."

"He may have acted wrongly," Qui-Gon said. "It is good that he recognized that before his own end. But I must ask you: What is its relevance to today, Queen Veda?" He asked the question, already knowing the answer.

"Elan is his daughter," Queen Veda answered quietly. "The past lives in the present always."

"And why have you told us this?" Qui-Gon asked.

"Because now I, too, am dying," the Queen answered. "Elan is my last secret. I want to do justice before I die, justice to Elan. She should know her birthright. She is the true heir to the throne, not Beju. She must have the Mark of the Crown on her," the Queen finished softly. Her gaze became unfocused again, as though she were back in the past.

"The Mark of the Crown?" Qui-Gon prompted.

"The mark of succession," Queen Veda explained. "It's not an actual mark on the body. Only the Council of Ministers can identify it."

"Prince Beju doesn't have it?" Qui-Gon asked.

"If what my husband said is true, he will not," the Queen replied. "It is not in the Council's best interests to test him. As you may imagine, most are not happy about the elections. Whoever becomes governor will have the right to open the Council to elections as well."

Qui-Gon nodded. The Council would naturally back Beju in order to retain their own power. "What would you like us to do?" he asked.

"I cannot contact Elan," the Queen said. "Obviously, she wouldn't meet with me. But if you could send a message to her and request a meeting . . . most do not refuse a Jedi request, you must admit. The hill people often jam communication to the outside. I could send someone with your message. Travel in the hill country is difficult and dangerous." The Queen looked down at her clasped hands. "And there's something else I haven't told you. The Council didn't want you to come. I had to negotiate with them. Under the terms of our agreement, you are forbidden to leave the city of Galu."

"That makes things more complicated," Qui-Gon observed neutrally.

"Yes, but not impossible," Queen Veda said eagerly. "Perhaps you can —"

Suddenly, the ornate metal door to the chamber was thrown open with such force that it hit the wall with a loud clang. Prince Beju strode in, with a tall, bald man in a silver robe at his side.

The Prince pointed a finger at Obi-Wan and Qui-Gon.

"You must leave Gala at once!" he cried.

The Queen rose to her feet. "Beju, explain yourself," she ordered, her voice shimmering with anger.

Beju slowly circled around the Jedi, his gaze contemptuous. He was a solidly built young man the same approximate height and weight as Obi-Wan, but with shoulder-length hair that was so pale it was almost white. His eyes were the same ice-blue as his mother's.

In his short encounter with the Prince, Obi-Wan had been granted a full picture of the boy's arrogance. He kept his own gaze steady but neutral. Qui-Gon was right. They should not antagonize the Prince any further.

"They call themselves Jedi, but they are nothing but troublemakers," Prince Beju spat out. "Have you heard about their doings on Phindar? They meddled and sowed discord. As a result, there was a great battle. Many were killed. Do you want that to happen on Gala, Mother?"

"They broke the back of a crime organization that had taken over the planet," Queen Veda replied calmly. "The Phindians are free. And they also brought us bacta to help with our own shortage."

The Prince flushed. "Some gift," he said contemptuously. "It was I who went to Phindar to negotiate the release of the bacta. Thanks to the Jedi, the bacta was off-loaded from my ship by the Phindian rebels! No doubt the Jedi ordered them to do so. And now they bring *my* bacta here as a gift? It is a joke!"

Obi-Wan stiffened. Why didn't Qui-Gon speak? The Prince was giving his own version of what happened on Phindar. It was filled with lies. Prince Beju knew that the Jedi had no proof that the Prince meant harm to Gala. Obi-Wan took note of his cleverness. But why wouldn't Qui-Gon speak the truth to Queen Veda?

The frail, bald man by Beju's side turned to the Jedi. "Do you have anything to say to this?"

"This is Lonnag Giba," Queen Veda said, turning to the Jedi. "He is the Head of the Council of Ministers, and graciously agreed to your visit."

"That was before I heard Prince Beju's

charges," Giba said sternly. "I ask you again, Jedi. What do you have to say?"

"We differ with the Prince about what happened on Phindar," Qui-Gon replied. His voice betrayed no irritation or anger at the Prince's charges. "But it would be pointless to argue. We were invited here. Why should we defend ourselves? If you wish us to leave your world, we shall."

"No!" Queen Veda exclaimed.

"Yes, Mother," Prince Beju said, flicking his cape behind him as he turned to face her. "Let them go. They are nothing but meddlers masquerading as guardians, weaklings masquerading as Knights."

Queen Veda sighed. "Enough, Beju," she said. "You have made your point. But Qui-Gon Jinn is right. The Jedi were invited here as guardians of the peace. We want the elections to go smoothly, don't we?"

"We don't want them at all," the Prince replied sullenly. "I am the true king of Gala. Father meant it to be so, and well you know it. If I ruled Gala, I would send these troublemakers on the first transport back to their so-holy Temple."

"Yet *I* am ruler now," the Queen said softly. "And I say they shall stay."

"Of course," the Prince said bitterly. "You deny me the crown. Why not deny me everything else?"

"Perhaps there is a compromise we can reach," Giba broke in smoothly. "The Jedi will remain on Gala. But they cannot leave the palace unescorted. We should send someone with them. Someone who knows the city well." He turned to the Jedi. "It is for your protection as well. The city is a dangerous place right now. There is much unrest. You'll need a guide."

Giba spoke diplomatically, but Obi-Wan didn't believe a word. The old man knew that Jedi didn't need help to defend themselves. It was just a way to get them to accept a spy who would report on their movements.

Obi-Wan waited for Qui-Gon's protest. But again, the Jedi Knight said nothing. How could he agree to such humiliating terms?

Queen Veda's gaze rested on her son for a moment. She looked tired — very tired. "As you wish, Beju," she said softly. "It is true. I cannot deny you everything." She wrapped her hand around a glowing rod that hung on the wall. It changed color to a soft blue. "Jono Dunn will escort the Jedi."

A moment later, the metal door opened. A

boy about Obi-Wan's age stood at attention, dressed in a navy tunic and pants.

"Jono Dunn, come forward," the Queen said. "These are the Jedi sent to Gala to oversee elections. Qui-Gon Jinn and Obi-Wan Kenobi. You will be their escort during their stay."

"They are not allowed to leave the palace without you," Prince Beju said quickly.

"Is this acceptable, Qui-Gon?" Queen Veda asked. Her eyes pleaded with him to agree.

Qui-Gon nodded. "We thank you for the assistance, Queen Veda," he said quietly.

Obi-Wan couldn't believe it. Not only was Qui-Gon accepting a guard, he was thanking the Queen!

Qui-Gon's sharp blue gaze moved to Giba. "And thank you, Giba. I'm sure our guard will protect us on the dangerous streets of Galu."

Qui-Gon put a hand on Jono Dunn's shoulder and positioned the boy between himself and Obi-Wan. Large and powerful, Qui-Gon towered over the slight boy. Although he was the same age, Obi-Wan's size and strength dwarfed the boy's as well. Qui-Gon had effortlessly made the point that Giba's offer was hollow. Jono was no protection for the Jedi. He was only a pawn in the game.

The Queen's lips quirked in a smile. Giba's

narrow face flushed red with anger. He pressed his thin lips together. "Enjoy your stay," he said through clenched teeth.

"I'm sure we shall," Qui-Gon responded.

Qui-Gon bowed and left the chamber. Obi-Wan followed only a second later. When he reached the hall, Qui-Gon was already gone.

Legacy.

The word struck a chord in Qui-Gon. He needed time to consider why it had lodged so deep within him. He took the exterior stairway to the gardens below. Obi-Wan would no doubt make his way to their quarters.

Trees were bursting with fruit, or were in blossom within the palace walls. Qui-Gon recognized a few — muja and tango. Masses of white, red, purple, and yellow marked the flower gardens beyond. The palace was famous for its extensive gardens. Qui-Gon knew that every plant, tree, and flower native to Gala was represented here. He strolled in the orchards. The muja trees were in blossom, and every sudden breeze sent a shower of pink petals drifting to the grass below.

The Queen had spoken of her legacy. Dying, she considered what she wished to leave behind. Her first thought was for her son. She even felt a bond with a stepchild she had never known.

The Galacians were a people of strong family bonds. Jobs and land were often passed down from parent to child. Marriages were carefully chosen to strengthen the family.

Qui-Gon had given up family and children for the life of a Jedi. He had chosen freely. No Jedi was bound to the life. He could choose to leave it at any time. Yet he knew he would not.

Qui-Gon leaned down to pick up petals from the grass. He let them drift through his fingers, to be carried by the wind. This would be his life, he thought. He would wander the galaxy. He would risk his life on behalf of strangers. What would he leave behind?

Qui-Gon's wandering took him to the kitchen gardens. Signs of planting surrounded him — shovels and rakes, careful rows of tiny seedlings taking root in the dirt. He looked down at the ground, almost surprised to see his own footprints there. Wind and rain would soon wash them away.

Elan had chosen to live apart from society. She followed a set of laws that belonged to no government, no world, only her fellow travelers.

She was like him, he realized. He had never met her, but he knew her.

"Qui-Gon?"

He turned at the sound of Obi-Wan's voice. The boy looked hesitant, afraid to disturb him.

"You disappeared," Obi-Wan said. "I didn't know where to look."

Qui-Gon could not share his thoughts. Obi-Wan was young, just starting out on his journey as a Jedi. He would not understand thoughts of legacies, of what he would leave behind. Not yet.

"Why did you agree to our not leaving the palace without an escort?" The question seemed torn from Obi-Wan's lips. Obviously, the boy thought Qui-Gon should have resisted Giba's suggestion.

"It is better for now that they think they can control us," Qui-Gon answered.

"Do you think the Queen is telling the truth?" Obi-Wan asked. "Does she really not want her son to win the election? And what does she want with Elan?"

"It could be as she says," Qui-Gon said slowly. "Or it could be that she wants us to lure Elan back here in order to kill her. Any Council member who was alive when the King was young knows that Beju is not the true heir. I would guess that Giba knows, for example. That is why he is afraid of us. There is always the danger that the secret will be exposed. Of course, if the Queen is lying about her intentions, she could be in league with Giba and their disagreement was staged for our benefit. If they can get rid of Elan, Queen Veda could call off the elections and appoint Beju King." Qui-Gon paused. "Or she could be lying about Elan for some other purpose we haven't discovered."

"Well, what do you believe?" Obi-Wan asked, trying to keep the confusion and impatience out of his voice.

"I think there are more secrets here," Qui-Gon answered thoughtfully. "Yet I think we should proceed as though the Queen is telling the truth. I am going to the hill country to find Elan."

"But our mission is to oversee the election!" Obi-Wan protested. "You can't do that from the hill country."

One corner of Qui-Gon's mouth lifted in a half smile. "You are sometimes a bit too fond of the rules, Obi-Wan. Things change. A mission is not clear-cut. Sometimes the direct road is not the one to take."

"But the safety of Gala is in our hands," Obi-Wan argued. "We were sent to be guardians of peace, not to go chasing long-lost daughters."

"You may disagree with me, Obi-Wan," Qui-Gon said mildly. "That is your right. But I will go."

"We're not allowed to leave the city, or even the palace without an escort," Obi-Wan reminded him. "You were the one to agree to it!

Giba and Prince Beju will be furious. Can't we allow the Queen's messenger to contact Elan?"

"Elan will not listen to a message," Qui-Gon replied. "She will have to be persuaded. She will have to see the truth in my eyes, or she will not come."

"You talk as if you know her!" Obi-Wan exclaimed.

"I do," Qui-Gon said quietly.

He walked closer to Obi-Wan and rested his hand gently on his shoulder for a moment. "Don't worry, Padawan. You can handle the mission here until I return. Be alert for palace intrigue." Qui-Gon's keen gaze swept the palace. "Trust no one here. There is a disturbance in the Force. I don't know where exactly it lies."

Obi-Wan looked at him, frustrated. "But what will I tell them when they ask where you are?"

Instead of answering, Qui-Gon strode through the half-planted gardens back to the trees. As he walked, he reached up and swiped a piece of ripe fruit from a branch overhead. Without turning, he tossed it over his shoulder. He didn't have to turn. He knew his Padawan would catch it.

"It's simple," he called behind him. "Tell them I'm still here."

"Respect is the cornerstone of the Master–Padawan bond," Obi-Wan said through his teeth. His voice bounced off the walls of his room, sounding hollow to his ears. Still, he needed the reminder. Every day, alone in the palace, he questioned Qui-Gon's decision.

The morning sun burnished the wood of the vast bed he slept in. A tapestry hung on the opposite wall, finely worked with metallic threads of gold, silver, and green. Woven blankets in rich, jewel-like colors kept out the night chill. It was the finest room he'd ever slept in. But staying in the palace for the past two days was no treat.

Qui-Gon had given him an impossible task. Each morning before dawn, Obi-Wan ran through the connecting door to Qui-Gon's quarters and disarranged the blankets on Qui-Gon's bed. He lay on his pillow to leave an indentation. Each morning Jono Dunn knocked on the door, bringing tea and fruit. Obi-Wan had told Jono that Qui-Gon meditated in the gardens early. He would wait for Jono to leave, then drink Qui-Gon's tea and eat his fruit as well as his own. That part was not hard. Obi-Wan was always hungry.

As for Prince Beju and Giba, Obi-Wan had to constantly invent excuses for Qui-Gon's absence. The Jedi was resting, or meditating, or touring the gardens. He would be along any minute, if they'd care to wait . . . they never did. He would take his evening meal in his room. He had already retired for the night. . . .

Perhaps they were suspicious. Obi-Wan couldn't tell. He had a feeling they were relieved that Qui-Gon wasn't more involved in the elections. Obi-Wan told Jono that Qui-Gon left much of the monitoring to him.

A soft knock came at Obi-Wan's door. A moment later, Jono opened it.

"I left a tray for Qui-Gon, as usual," Jono said. He placed Obi-Wan's tray on the small table by the window. Usually, he bowed and left quickly, but today, he lingered.

"I did not see him in the gardens," he said. "It's my job to pick the flowers for the Queen morning and night. Yet I never see the Jedi."

Obi-Wan reached for a piece of blumfruit.

"The gardens are so large. He most likely avoided you. He doesn't like to be interrupted during his morning meditation."

Jono stood quietly. He was a handsome boy, with golden hair and the glowing skin of the Galacians. Although he had accompanied Obi-Wan on several trips to inspect polling places in Galu, he had not talked much.

"You think I am a spy," he burst out suddenly. "You think I am working for the Prince."

"Well, aren't you?" Obi-Wan asked calmly.

"I do not report to the Prince," Jono said scornfully. "I serve the Queen. The Dunns have served the ruler of Gala since the Tallah dynasty began."

"So you come from a line of royal servants?" Obi-Wan asked curiously. He pushed the plate of food toward Jono.

Jono ignored it. He raised his chin proudly. "The Dunns are great landowners far from Galu. I was chosen at the age of five to come to the palace. It was a great honor. All children in the Dunn family line are watched from an early age. Only the smartest and quickest are chosen."

Obi-Wan held out a piece of fruit toward Jono. "I, too, was chosen at an early age," he told the boy. "I left my family and went to the Jedi Temple. It was a great honor. But I missed my family very much, even though I couldn't really remember them."

Jono reached out a tentative hand and took the fruit from Obi-Wan. "The beginning was the hardest," he said, popping it into his mouth.

"The Jedi Temple is calm and beautiful. It is my home, and yet it is not a *home,* like everyone else has."

"That's just the way I feel!" Jono agreed, sitting on the edge of the bed next to Obi-Wan. "The palace was too grand at first. And I missed the smell of the sea. But now I feel at home. I know my duty, and I am proud to do it. There is honor in serving my Queen." He met Obi-Wan's gaze steadily. "But I do not spy."

At that moment, Obi-Wan and Jono became friends. Jono continued to accompany him on his walks through Galu, but instead of silently staying a short pace behind him, Jono walked beside Obi-Wan, sharing stories of the city and of Deca Brun, his hero.

"The Queen is right to call for elections," Jono told him. "Deca Brun will help Gala to rise again. He is for all the people, not just rich people."

Jono never asked again about Qui-Gon. Obi-Wan knew Jono suspected that Qui-Gon had left the palace. He appreciated his guide's silence. He did not have to lie to Jono any longer. His friend asked no questions.

Jono often spoke of his family. Even though he rarely saw them, his connection to them was strong. Obi-Wan came to envy Jono's deep commitment. He had left behind a concept of family when he took up his destiny as a Jedi. His allegiance was to the Jedi Code. Was this choice the right one? Suddenly the Jedi Code seemed so much more abstract than the ties of blood.

Heritage. Legacies. He wished he could speak of what he was feeling to Qui-Gon. But his Master wouldn't understand. He was deeply committed to the Jedi Code. He did not look back and wonder what he was missing.

And besides, he had abandoned Obi-Wan in order to chase a ghost.

Evenings were long in Gala. The sun set early, and the three moons rose slowly in the navy sky. Obi-Wan liked to walk in the orchard at that hour, when the pale gleam of moonlight turned the fruit on the trees to silver.

One evening he was surprised to find Queen Veda sitting on the grass, her back against the thick, multistemmed trunk of a muja tree. She wasn't wearing her headdress, and her pale gold hair spilled down to her waist. She looked like a young girl until Obi-Wan drew closer and saw the wasting of illness on her face.

"Sit down, young Obi-Wan," she said, gesturing next to her. "I, too, like the orchard at this time."

Obi-Wan sat next to her, cross-legged and erect in Jedi fashion. He had not seen the Queen since he'd arrived. She looked shockingly worse.

"I like the smell of the grass," Queen Veda murmured, running her hands through it. "Before I was sick, I used to like to look at it from my window. I looked at everything from a window. Now I find I must touch it and smell it and be part of it." She placed a bit of grass in Obi-Wan's palm and closed his fingers over it. "Hold on to life, Obi-Wan. That is my only piece of advice to you."

Obi-Wan saw the marks of tears on the Queen's face. He wished Qui-Gon were here. His Master's calm compassion soothed even the most fevered hearts. What would Qui-Gon say?

He would start with something neutral, but sympathetic. He would let the Queen speak, knowing she needed a willing space to talk.

"You are not feeling better," he said carefully.

"No, I am feeling worse," Queen Veda said, resting her head against the trunk. "The pain is very bad at night. I can't sleep. By the middle of the day I feel somewhat better, but at night it begins again. That's why I come out here, before the pain gets bad. I want to remember days I felt well. Days in the country . . ." The Queen sighed.

"In the country?" Obi-Wan prompted.

"The Tallahs have a country estate west of here," Queen Veda said. "Just after I had fallen ill I went there to recuperate. Maybe it was the fresh air. Or maybe," she said ruefully, "it was being able to rest. No Council of Ministers calling me to meetings. No servants to buzz around me. Just the caretaker and myself. But then it seemed the government could not run without me, so they came to me. Within days, I felt worse than ever. That was the worst thing," she said sadly. "To feel that I was getting better, and then to relapse."

"But why don't you return?" Obi-Wan asked.

"The elections consumed my time at first," the Queen said. "Now I am too weak to travel. So my doctors tell me. And they are the best in Galu. Every day has been the same for me. Hope that I am recovering. Then despair. Now hope is gone. I'm just waiting."

Obi-Wan looked at her. The moons had risen higher, painting her pale face with a silvery cast. He saw again that she had once been beautiful.

"Don't look so sad," she told him. "I've accepted it at last. Now, will you help me rise? It's time for my tea."

Obi-Wan rose and held out his hand. Her grip was weak. He placed another hand under her elbow and helped her stand.

"Good night, Queen Veda," he told her as she moved off, her gown a whisper in the grass. "I'm sorry," he added softly, knowing she would not hear.

The Queen's words had moved him. Whether she was lying about wanting Elan to have her birthright, he didn't know. But he knew the Queen had spoken honestly about her illness and her fears. He could only imagine how terrible it must be to feel as though you are slowly losing your grip on life. To suffer, to feel better, and then to have that hope of life snatched away every evening as the moons rose. . . .

Every evening. Obi-Wan sat up straighter. The Force was telling him to focus. Wasn't there an odd rhythm to the Queen's illness? And hadn't she said she had felt better at her country estate?

Until the Council members arrived . . .

The thought made Obi-Wan dizzy.

Was the Queen being poisoned?

Obi-Wan didn't hesitate. If his suspicions were true, there was no time to lose. Quickly, he rose to his feet and hurried through the gardens. He spied an old man dressed in the silver robes of a council member strolling through the trees, placing an occasional hand on the silver bark for support. His milky blue eyes were turned upward toward the moon. Obi-Wan doubled back before he was seen. He did not want to attract any attention.

He sped noiselessly through the palace hallways to the Queen's chambers. He knocked softly on the door.

"It's Obi-Wan," he called.

Jono opened the door. "The Queen is taking her nightly refreshment," he said.

"Who brings it?" Obi-Wan asked. When Jono looked puzzled, he added quickly, "I was wondering if I could get some tea and something to eat at night."

"The kitchen servants bring it up," Jono answered. "I'll ask them to include you." He grinned. "I'll make sure you get the cook's best sweets."

"May I see the Queen?" Obi-Wan asked. "I just need a word or two."

Jono nodded and withdrew to an inner chamber. After a moment, the door opened, and he beckoned Obi-Wan in.

The Queen was reclining on a sleep-couch, a tray with a teacup and a plate of fruit and sweets next to her on a small table. A small bouquet of flowers stood next to it.

"I wanted to make sure you were all right," Obi-Wan said, coming closer. "You seemed tired in the orchard."

"How kind of you." The Queen gave him a sad smile. "I'm a bit more tired than usual, I'm afraid. But don't worry about me, Obi-Wan Kenobi. You have more important matters to attend to."

"I think not," he said gently. "Your well-being is very important to me, Queen Veda."

He reached down and felt the teacup. There was only a small amount left. "Your tea is cold. Can I fetch you another?"

The Queen's eyes fluttered closed. "I've had enough," she said weakly. "You can tell Jono to take it away."

"You rest now," Obi-Wan said gently. He picked up the tray and moved to the doorway. When he slipped through, the outer chamber was empty. Good. He did not want to involve Jono in his plans.

Quickly, he carried the tray to his room. There, he poured the tea into an empty vial from his emergency medpac. He placed the vial and the rest of the sweets in a drawstring bag and slipped them into a pocket of his tunic. Then he brought the tray back down to the kitchens.

Tomorrow, he would have to find a substance analyzer. And he would have to do it without involving Jono.

"I'm worried about my Queen," Jono told Obi-Wan the next day as they walked down the streets of Galu. "I watch her grow weaker by the day. There is nothing the doctors can do. Nothing I can do."

"You are close to her," Obi-Wan observed. He had seen the affectionate way the Queen spoke to Jono. He certainly got more warmth from the Queen than Obi-Wan did from Qui-Gon. But then, Jono had served her now for eight years.

Jono bit his lip. He nodded. "It is so hard. Prince Beju doesn't come to see her. He's angry at her. And he says it upsets him to see her look so ill. He needs to focus on the election. How can a son be so cruel? He thinks only of his own feelings!"

They stopped outside a polling area that had been set up in a community hall. Obi-Wan had toured many of the polling areas in Galu. He spoke to those who would direct the voters to the private datapad terminals to cast their votes. He tested the datapads for accuracy. But he felt as though his visits were useless. He was not an expert on voting processes.

On his first outing, he had contacted Qui-Gon by comlink to tell him how useless he felt. Qui-Gon had no sympathy.

"Your presence is enough," he said shortly. "Just let them see that the process is being monitored from an outside source. That will give the people trust in the system."

Obi-Wan turned to Jono. "Jono, would you mind waiting outside? I think it would be better. After all, people know you're a palace worker. I have to look neutral or they won't trust the voting."

"That's true," Jono said hesitantly. "But I am supposed to stay at your side. . . ." His voice trailed off, but he smiled. "Of course you're right, Obi-Wan. I wouldn't want to jeopardize the elections. I'll wait over there in the plaza."

Obi-Wan thanked him and walked into the community center. He felt guilty deceiving Jono this way. But he couldn't involve his friend in his task. If the Queen was being poisoned, no one at the palace could find out that he knew. He had to trap the poisoner. If he needed Jono's help later, he would ask for it. First, he would need to consult Qui-Gon.

Obi-Wan headed through the community center and out a side door. He quickly walked down an alley into a side street. Then he doubled back in the opposite direction.

On the way to the center, Obi-Wan had kept his eye out for info-data booths. They were dotted around Galu, and citizens used them to look up information on services available in the capital. There was one only a few blocks from the center.

The bright green light on top of the info-data booth glowed, telling him the booth was free. Quickly, Obi-Wan entered. He typed "substance analyzer" into the datapad. Within seconds, the screen flashed with several names. Obi-Wan accessed a city map, which pinpointed where each analyzer was located. One name, Mali Errat, had a lab close to Obi-Wan's location. He touched the screen, and a luminous green path showed him the route.

Obi-Wan hurried through the crowded streets. Jono would soon start to wonder why he was taking so long. The boy knew the streets of Galu well, and might search for him.

There was no answer to his knock at the address, and no sign outside. Obi-Wan pushed open the door cautiously and found himself in a tiny, cluttered room. One long durasteel table ran across the middle of it, touching the walls at both ends. The table was covered with equipment: tubes, vials, datapads, circuits, measuring devices, holofiles. Metal storage boxes crowded the floor, some stacked precariously, almost as high as the ceiling. Durasheets covered with data unfurled across the floor.

Was this a lab, or a storage area for a lunatic?

"Hello?" Obi-Wan asked.

"Who's that?" A head popped up from behind a stack of storage boxes. It was a Galacian elder. Wisps of platinum hair covered his bald head, and his pale green eyes squinted at Obi-Wan. "What is it? Come on, then," he said impatiently, snapping his fingers. "State your business."

Obi-Wan walked closer and peered around the boxes. The man was sitting on the floor.

Data printouts were littered around him and coiled in his lap. "I'm looking for Mali Errat —"

"Speak up, boy, don't whisper!"

"Mali Errat," Obi-Wan repeated, louder this time.

"Don't shout! I'm Mali. You look surprised to find me in my own lab, boy. Well, what do you want?"

"I have something I need analyzed —" Obi-Wan started.

Mali interrupted him again. "Another surprise. You're in a substance analysis lab. Therefore I would assume you have something to be analyzed. Obviously, I am brighter than I look." The old man chortled.

Obi-Wan looked at the cluttered lab, the rolls of data printout that coiled on the floor like snakes. "Maybe you're too busy —"

"Way too busy, it's true," Mali snapped. "So don't waste my time. Show me your item."

He didn't really have a choice. There was no time to find a more conventional scientist. Or a more polite one. Obi-Wan withdrew the pouch from his tunic. He handed it to Mali.

Mali took out the vial of tea and the little round sweet cakes. "You want me to analyze your lunch?"

Obi-Wan held out his hand. "I can go elsewhere."

"Touchy young man," Mali muttered. "When do you need results?"

"Right now," Obi-Wan said.

"It will cost you," Mali warned.

"I have credits," Obi-Wan said, showing him.

Mali took several credits from his hand. "That will do. Now." He stood. He was a small man, but still agile, Obi-Wan noted as Mali leaped over a storage box and pulled a stool up to the durasteel table.

Whistling through his teeth, Mali first took some crumbs from the cakes and inserted them into a scan grid.

"Cake," he pronounced after a moment, reading the data. "Sweetener, muja, meal, coagulate . . ."

"Nothing else?" Obi-Wan asked.

Mali licked the residue off his fingers. "It's delicious." He popped the rest into his mouth.

Obi-Wan sighed. "Try the liquid."

Mali poured a drop from the vial into a scan grid. Seconds later, the grid flashed a graph with numbers and symbols.

"Ah," Mali murmured, straightening. "Fascinating."

"What is it?" Obi-Wan asked, leaning forward.

"Tea," Mali said.

"And?" Obi-Wan prompted.

"Water," Mali answered.

"And?" Obi-Wan asked.

Mali squinted at him. "Young impatient man, you must tell me what I am looking for. There are herbal compounds here, some acids, some tannins. But nothing I can tell is out of the ordinary. Unless you tell me what out of the ordinary event you are suspecting."

"Poison," Obi-Wan said reluctantly.

"Well, there you are! Always better to say what you want at the outset. Otherwise, we waste time. No poison in the cake. A good thing, eh? I ate it!" Humming, Mali stared at the graph again. He pressed a few keys on the analyzer. Another graph appeared, then a stream of numbers and symbols.

"Well?" Obi-Wan asked.

"Interesting," Mali said. "There is one substance that's not identifiable."

"Is that unusual?" Obi-Wan asked.

He shrugged. "Yes, but not too. It's just a matter of searching other data fields for chemical compounds with the same structure. But that takes time."

"I don't have time," Obi-Wan said grimly.

Mali looked at the vial. He let out a whistle through his teeth. "Ah. I see your point. I still have to search, impatient young man. But for another credit, I will search fast."

Obi-Wan handed him the credit. He started

for the door, then turned. "Can't you tell me if it *could* be poison?" he asked. "Just your educated guess."

"It's possible," Mali admitted. "I can tell you this, young man. Whatever it is, it doesn't belong in tea."

Before finding Jono, Obi-Wan found a secluded back alley to use his comlink to contact Qui-Gon. He didn't want to risk using the comlink in public. And he felt safer contacting Qui-Gon outside of the palace walls.

He waited for long minutes. But Qui-Gon did not respond. He was out of reach.

Obi-Wan was on his own.

He trudged back to the community center. Jono was sitting on top of the wall that circled the plaza. His eyes were closed, his face tilted to catch the warming rays of the sun. The sun shines for such a short time during the Galacian day that Galacians take any opportunity to sunbathe.

"Sorry to take so long," Obi-Wan told Jono. "There were a few problems. Nothing major."

Jono jumped down from his perch. "I knew you would return. It's all right. I am used to waiting. I have waited for a friend for a long time, Obi-Wan."

CHAPTER 7

The Queen had not exaggerated the difficult journey to find the hill people. At first, the roads had been clearly marked. Qui-Gon had found a ride in a speeder to the outskirts of the city. A kind farmer had taken him far on a turbo cart, a young teenager on his speeder bike. But as the roads grew worse and the landscape more desolate, there were no more rides to be had.

The hills rose before him on the third day. They were rugged and steep, climbing through dense forests. Occasionally he would come to a clearing and be met with the eerie sight of a group of large standing stones. The harsh beauty of the land grew as he traveled higher. The short days ended in sunsets that turned the sky to blazing colors. Then the three moons rose, casting a silvery glow over the pale rocks and twisted trees.

His comlink no longer worked. Qui-Gon hoped that Obi-Wan would not get into trouble back at the palace. He was anxious to find Elan, anxious to get back to Galu.

He reached the summit of the first range of hills. Snow dotted the peaks. The only way through was a series of narrow passes. Qui-Gon felt exposed and vulnerable as he hiked through the narrow gorge.

As he traveled, the sky darkened. The temperature dropped, and he unpacked his thermal cape from his survival pack. He could smell snow in the air. A storm was heading this way. He would have to find shelter soon.

Perhaps it was because his eyes were constantly moving, searching for shelter. Perhaps it was because the eerie silence pressed on him, the dark sky like a lowering curtain. Because Qui-Gon might not have caught the flicker of movement to his left if every sense hadn't been on alert. It could have been no more than a shadow flickering on a rock, or the stir of a leaf. But the movement had caught his eye and prepared him just a few quick seconds before the attack came.

The bandits zoomed down on landspeeders with mounted ion cannons on front and rear. Qui-Gon tossed his survival pack on the ground.

He activated his lightsaber just in time to meet the first speeder. He dodged at the last possible second, sending the speeder careening into a tree. He was already turning to his left to slash at the driver of the second speeder. His blow connected, and the speeder lurched to the left, the driver hanging on as it barely missed the canyon wall. He righted it at the last second and zoomed back up to come around from the right.

Qui-Gon dove for cover. He could use the fact that he was in such a narrow space. They would have to come at him one at a time. While the speeders maneuvered to come at him again, he found a boulder close to a grouping of massive standing stones. The canyon was to his back, the stones to his left. The bandits could only approach from the right.

There were ten speeders . . . no, twelve — two more buzzed down from the sky. One came at him, ion cannons blasting. Chips of stone flew at him as he ducked and rolled, and stood again as the speeder zoomed past him. Qui-Gon used the momentum of his roll to slash at the driver from behind. He fell off the speeder, which zoomed out of control and crashed. The driver lay on the ground, unable to rise.

The second speeder was down, and the next one was right on its heels, cannons firing. This driver was more skilled than the others. He zigzagged from side to side, the cannon fire missing Qui-Gon by centimeters as he took cover from standing stone to standing stone. He reached out for the Force. He needed it.

He felt it pulse around him, grow stronger. He drew it in.

He moved quickly, surprising the driver. He flattened himself on the ground as the driver overshot him, cannons shooting at the canyon wall now. He counted off seconds as the driver made a sharp turn to come back at him again. Qui-Gon left the cover of the stones and stood, lightsaber held high. This time, he aimed at the speeder's control panel. He struck a hard blow that he felt all the way up to his shoulder.

The pain shot up his arm. The blow had cost him, but it disabled the speeder. The engine began to smoke, and the speeder tilted wildly. It hit the speeder bearing down on Qui-Gon. They both crashed to the canyon floor.

Then Qui-Gon saw the speeder off to his left. The driver was either reckless or skilled — it remained to be seen. He was coming fast, straight at the standing stones. The gap between them was small, barely enough for a speeder to fit through. They were spaced at irregular intervals, making it almost impossible to navigate between them.

Almost is the key word, Qui-Gon realized too late.

The daring driver made a hard left, turning the speeder sideways. It zoomed through the small opening. He reversed, hovered in midair, then made a sharp turn to the right. He zoomed through the next opening, barely clearing it. Now he had a split second to make a clear shot at Qui-Gon.

The Force helped Qui-Gon move, sending him leaping up on top of the boulder he had first used for cover. Another speeder was already bearing down on him. The driver was surprised by the sudden move, and made a hard turn to avoid Qui-Gon, even as his cannon boomed. At the same time, the driver midway through the standing stones fired his cannons. The two blasts collided in midair, sending an explosive charge that ricocheted off the boulder. The impact turned the boulder into a bomb, shattering it into large pieces of shrapnel that seemed to fly at Qui-Gon in slow motion.

Qui-Gon was hit in the chest. Badly. The impact knocked him backward, his lightsaber leaving his grip and flying meters away from him. He lay on his back, stunned. He could hear the engines of the speeders roaring as the two vehicles maneuvered to take their next shot.

His mind whirled from his fall. He groped for his lightsaber. He knew one thing: He was caught between the two blasting cannons, out in the open. He called on the Force and summoned his lightsaber to his hand.

The higher whine of a new engine came to his ears. As his lightsaber flew to his grip, Qui-Gon saw another vehicle zoom into the tight spaces among the standing stones. He recognized it as a swoop, a speeder bike with a powerful engine. The controls were located on the handlebars and on the saddle. Only the most daring riders could master such a vehicle. Just a slight touch could send it careening out of control.

He'd thought the first bandit was daring. The swoop driver bordered on reckless. But Qui-Gon read confidence and control in the way the vehicle moved, so fast it was almost a blur, banking right and left, hovering in midair and then reversing, zooming high and low to maneuver underneath the larger speeder.

Qui-Gon pushed himself to his feet. The pain hit him, red and searing, and he realized he'd been hit by a chunk of boulder in the leg as well. He called on the Force to help his body to respond, his mind to clear. The speeder was bearing down on him again. He leaped to avoid cannon fire and somersaulted over the low-flying speeder, striking down as he did so at the control panel. He heard the engine sputter and die, and the speeder crashed.

Qui-Gon hit the ground and dodged blaster fire from a pilot hurrying to help his comrade in the standing stones. But this driver was not so adept. He attempted to turn into the small gap and missed, hitting the stone and sending his craft wobbling as he struggled to right it.

Qui-Gon got a good look at the driver of the swoop. He wore a black cloth headdress that wrapped around his face. Only his eyes were visible. His gloved hands gripped the handlebars of the swoop as he expertly twisted and turned through the stones, running the speeder down relentlessly. Yet Qui-Gon could tell that the swoop driver was careful to allow the speeder enough maneuverability so that it wouldn't crash amid the stones.

Qui-Gon wondered what would happen to him once the swoop driver took care of the bandit on the speeder. The driver was surely a bandit, too. Qui-Gon would probably have his hands full again.

The remaining speeders hovered, reluctant to help their comrade in the maze of standing stones, distracted from Qui-Gon for the moment. Qui-Gon stood, his lightsaber activated and at his side. He was ready.

At last the speeder made it through the standing stones, the swoop now so close that it was almost touching the speeder's tailpipe. Suddenly, the swoop turned and flanked the speeder, driving it toward Qui-Gon.

Qui-Gon was surprised by the maneuver but not unprepared. He leaped aside as ion cannons began to fire. He could feel that his leg wound made him clumsy. He stumbled slightly, then twisted to keep the speeder in view.

The driver of the swoop kept one hand on the controls and picked up a bowcaster with the other. Effortlessly keeping the swoop on track flanking the speeder, he aimed and shot at the driver. The laser hit the driver in the wrist. Qui-Gon saw his mouth open in a howl that turned into a snarl.

The distraction was all he needed. Qui-Gon summoned the Force. He needed one last burst. The Force propelled him in a flying leap to the top of one of the standing stones. He delivered a stunning blow to the surprised speeder driver as he zoomed past. The speeder crashed into the canyon floor.

Qui-Gon leaped down from the exposed position. He heard the high whine of other swoops. He looked up and saw them like black insects against the gray sky, heading straight for him. There were at least twenty, and more were heading down the pass from the opposite direction.

He would not be able to fight so many. Qui-Gon watched as the speeder bandits took off. Some of the swoops gave chase. Had he landed in the middle of a bandit war?

The lead swoop flew toward him. Its repulsorlift engines kept it airborne a few inches off the ground as the driver leaped off, his bowcaster pointed straight at Qui-Gon.

There was no use fighting. Qui-Gon deactivated his lightsaber and waited.

"Who are you?" The voice was gruff. Qui-Gon was surprised at how young the bandit sounded.

"Qui-Gon Jinn. I am a Jedi Knight sent to contact someone."

The bowcaster was now pointed at his heart. "Who?" the bandit demanded.

Qui-Gon decided that it would do no harm to let the bandits know his mission. Perhaps they could be bargained with.

"The leader of the hill people," he said. "Elan."

Slowly, the bandit unraveled the black headdress. A shower of silvery hair spilled over slender shoulders. A young woman stood before him. Her eyes were dark, the color of an evening sky, unusual for a Galacian. Her impatient gaze flicked over him, taking in everything about him and making it clear she was not impressed a bit.

"Well, at least you did something right," she said. "You've found me."

CHAPTER 8

Elan tossed the headdress and bowcaster into the side compartment of her swoop. She dusted off her hands on her trousers. "The standing stones are sacred to the hill people," she told Qui-Gon. "You almost destroyed them."

"I did not mean to."

"You chose the field of battle," Elan said crisply.

"I needed cover," Qui-Gon said.

Snowflakes began to twinkle down from the sky. Elan cocked an eyebrow at him. "Ever hear of boulders? Trees?"

Qui-Gon resisted the temptation to argue. She was deliberately putting him on the defensive. "Do you know the attackers?" he asked instead.

She shrugged. "Bandits from the city outskirts. They make raids up here occasionally.

There are always rumors in Galu that the hill people hoard gold. The greedy fools think it's true. I wish they'd leave us alone. We don't bother them." She gazed at him stonily. "Who sent you to find me, and why?"

"Queen Veda sent me," Qui-Gon said.

She waved a dismissive hand. "Then go back to Galu. I don't recognize her authority."

"Don't you want to know what she wants?"

Elan crossed to the swoop and swung a leg over the saddle. "Something about the election, I'm sure. It's no concern of mine." She pointed back the way Qui-Gon had come. "The way back is that way. Don't stay in the hills. You'll be sorry if you do."

He didn't know if she was threatening him, or warning him against other bandit attacks. Another swoop flew toward them and stopped, hovering in the air. A tall young man with bluish skin gave Qui-Gon a quick glance, then turned to Elan. "Bad storm coming."

"I know, Dana," Elan said, casting a worried eye at the sky. "When they come in, they come in hard."

As if to illustrate her words, the snowfall suddenly began. The flakes were like hard crystals, peppering Qui-Gon's exposed skin. He leaned over to retrieve the survival pack he'd dropped when the fight began. The pain cut him to the quick, and he let out an involuntary hiss.

"He's wounded," Dana said.

Elan frowned, annoyed. "I can't send you back, I suppose. Wounded, with this storm. You'd never survive. And night falls quickly in the mountains."

Qui-Gon waited. His wounds hurt him. But they would heal. Now it appeared that he was lucky to have them. Elan's conscience wouldn't allow her to send him on alone.

"One night," she warned him. "That's all. Now climb up behind me. And don't fall off. I don't want to have to rescue you again."

The hill people weren't overly friendly, but they were kind. Their encampment was made up of white domes of various sizes constructed out of a flexible material that was bolted to struts. Inside his small dome, Qui-Gon found every comfort and convenience — thick carpets and quilts, a glowing heater, a small kitchen and bath, even a datapad for his personal use.

Dana told him that a healer would come to dress his wounds. Qui-Gon did the best he could himself, but he could not reach the gash he'd received on his back when he fell. He slipped out of his tunic and waited for the healer to arrive. Even though the storm howled outside, the dome felt solid and warm.

There was a knock on the dome door, and he called out for the person to enter.

Elan ducked through the doorway, carrying a small bag. She shut it quickly behind her to keep out the wind and snow. "Good, you're ready," she said.

"You're the healer?" Qui-Gon asked, surprised.

She nodded as she set out vials of ointment and rolls of bandages. When she looked at him, her blunt gaze was challenging. "Surprised? I'm not the healing type, is that it?"

"No, that's not it," Qui-Gon answered. "I have just never known a healer who could pilot a swoop like that."

A reluctant grin tugged at her mouth. "All right, let's see what we have here." She inspected his wounds and dabbed more ointment on one, then dressed it. "You did a good job."

"Jedi are trained as healers, too," Qui-Gon said. "I can't reach the one on my back."

"Turn around."

Qui-Gon felt the coolness as she dabbed salve on his wound. The salve soothed the burning. "Thank you for such comfortable quarters," he said.

"We do not live like barbarians, no matter what the city people think," Elan answered. She unrolled a bandage.

"I didn't think you did," Qui-Gon said. "And it has been my experience on many worlds that ignorance breeds fear. The fearful make up stories about what they fear."

"Yes," Elan said coolly. "The city people are ignorant and fearful. I agree. So why would I want to live among them?"

Qui-Gon tried to curb his exasperation. Talking with Elan was like trying to catch a drifting snowflake. Whatever he said, she found a way to make his meaning disappear.

"So that is why you won't participate in the elections?" Qui-Gon asked. "The support of the hill people could make a difference to the right candidate."

"And who is the right candidate?" Elan asked. She still worked on the bandage on his back, so he couldn't see her face. He could only feel her cool, expert fingers and occasionally the brush of her hair against his skin. "Deca Brun, who shouts slogans and murmurs promises? Wila Prammi, who has been a slave to the royal system and now talks of democracy? That young fool, Prince Beju? No thank you, Jedi. I don't trust the elections, I don't trust the Queen, and I don't trust the candidates. I am happy where I am." She patted the bandage in place, then rose. "I'm finished."

Qui-Gon turned to face her. "Thank you. You feel no loyalty to Gala?"

She replaced the vials and bandages in her bag with quick motions. "I feel loyalty to my own people. I can trust them."

"What about your world?" Qui-Gon asked, easing back into his tunic. "Gala is about to undergo a great change. A good change. Shouldn't the hill people be part of it?"

Elan picked up her bag. She turned to him impatiently. "Is that why the Queen sent you? To ask for my support for her son?"

"No," Qui-Gon said quietly. He watched her face carefully. "She sent me to tell you that Prince Beju is not King Cana's true heir."

"And why should she tell me this?" Elan demanded. "And why should I care?"

"Because you are the heir," Qui-Gon said. "You are King Cana's daughter."

Elan blinked. He saw the shock on her face, and saw how she was trying to control it.

"What lies are these?" she asked, taking a step backward. "Why did you come here?"

"Lies or truth, perhaps only you can discover," Qui-Gon said. "I only say what has been told to me, and what I've come to believe. Queen Veda recently discovered that King Cana had a child before he married her. That child is you. The Queen says she wants you to know your birthright."

"This is a trick," Elan said flatly. "A trick to lure me back to the city. She wants to imprison me, scatter the hill people —"

"No," Qui-Gon interrupted firmly. "I believe she only wants you to know. That is all."

Elan whirled around, her pale silver hair flying. She stalked toward the door. "I won't listen to this."

"What about your parents?" Qui-Gon asked, raising his voice to be heard above the howling wind. "Your mother?"

Elan turned to face him again. "It is none of your business, Jedi. But I'll tell you so that you will not try to confuse me with lies again. My mother lived in the hills all her life. She never went to Galu. My father was a great healer, renowned by all the hill people. You are wrong."

"I am sure that those who raised you are worthy people," Qui-Gon said. "But Cana's blood may be in you, Elan."

She stared at him icily. "Perhaps you actually believe the Queen's lies. But Qui-Gon, I tell you that there is a plan behind her words. It is up to you to find it out."

"She is dying," Qui-Gon said quietly. "She is

thinking of her legacy. It is a gift she gives to you."

"I don't believe it, and I don't want it," Elan answered firmly. "This is my legacy." She gestured to take in the dome and all that was outside it. "These are my people. We are all outcasts. You've seen how Gala is ruled by powerful families. The hill people began a hundred years ago when those who were different — whose eyes were too dark, whose skin was too dark, who had no family — took refuge here. We made our own society, and freedom is our first rule. My parents gave me this heritage. I am proud of it. I don't want any crown."

"You make a large decision in a very short time," Qui-Gon observed.

Her dark eyes studied him. "And what is this to you, Qui-Gon Jinn?" she asked softly. "You have come a long way, almost lost your life, just to tell me this. But Gala is not your world. Its people are not your people. I have ties to something. Do you? Why should I listen to talk of legacies from someone who has no ties?"

Qui-Gon fell silent. Elan was trying to wound him. Some of what she said merely echoed his own thoughts.

"My comlink was not working earlier," Qui-

Gon said. "Is there any way I can contact my apprentice in Galu?"

"We jam communications in the hills for our protection," Elan answered. "But we will let you contact him as soon as the storm lessens. Speak to Dana."

She opened the door. The fierce wind blew back her hair and clothes and sent an icy draft toward Qui-Gon. Elan didn't flinch.

"Tell your apprentice that when the weather clears, you will be on your way," she added. Then she ducked out into the storm.

The door banged shut behind her. He had come a long way for nothing. His mission had failed.

Obi-Wan's comlink was activated when he woke the next day. Qui-Gon had contacted him at last. Afraid to use it in his room — he was still wary of surveillance — he took it to a corner of the gardens that was planted with wild tropical species. Under cover of the thick leaves of overhanging trees, he opened the communication line.

"Hello, Obi-Wan." Qui-Gon's voice sounded strained. Obi-Wan sensed something . . .

"You're wounded, Master," he said in concern.

"I'm healing now. I ran into some bandits," Qui-Gon explained. "But I found the hill people as well."

"And Elan?"

"I found her," Qui-Gon said. "My masked rescuer turned out to be the one I sought. But I haven't had much success. She thinks the

Queen is lying to further some plan of her own."

"That could be true," Obi-Wan said.

"And you?" Qui-Gon asked. "Have you discovered anything?"

"I think the Queen is being poisoned," Obi-Wan said. Hurriedly, he explained his suspicions and his visit to the substance analysis lab.

Qui-Gon's face grew grave. "This is very bad news," he said.

"Who could it be?" Obi-Wan asked.

"Ask yourself who would benefit from her death," Qui-Gon said. "If she dies, the elections could be suspended by her successor."

"Beju!" Obi-Wan cried. "But would he poison his own mother?"

"He might," Qui-Gon said. "Though I don't think so. I think under his anger there is genuine affection."

"I'm not so sure," Obi-Wan muttered. He didn't have a very good opinion of the Prince.

"Or it could be someone who wants the royal line to continue," Qui-Gon continued. "Like Giba. Or it could be someone whose motive isn't obvious. You must be careful, Padawan. You must have proof. Maybe when the substance analyzer gives you the poisonous agent, you will be able to figure out the culprit.

Didn't you say that Jono brought the nightly tea?"

"It can't be him," Obi-Wan said. "He only picks it up in the kitchens and delivers it."

"You sound very sure of your new friend," Qui-Gon replied neutrally. "But sometimes the obvious is the answer."

"I am sure of him," Obi-Wan said. Annoyance rose in him at Qui-Gon's suggestion. His Master had chosen to leave Obi-Wan in charge at the palace. Why couldn't Qui-Gon trust his judgment?

"In the meantime, you must warn the Queen," Qui-Gon said. "I see no other way. She must only take food from those she trusts. Better yet, she should prepare it herself."

"Are you coming back soon?" Obi-Wan hoped the answer would be yes.

"In a few days. My wounds might prevent me from traveling."

"But you said you were healing!" Obi-Wan protested.

"But they don't know that. Elan won't take well to hearing that her healing arts are slow. She is proud of her skills."

"Elan is a healer?" Obi-Wan asked. A thought struck him. "But that means she could know about such things as poisons."

Qui-Gon's tone turned stern. "That is quite a jump in logic, Padawan. Are you saying Elan could have something to do with the Queen's illness? She never comes to Galu."

"But we don't know that," Obi-Wan argued. "You said she was in disguise when you met her. What if she had knowledge of her position as heir? You asked me who would benefit from the Queen's death. Isn't Elan that person?"

"She didn't know she was the heir," Qui-Gon said shortly.

"Or so she pretended," Obi-Wan said stubbornly. If Qui-Gon could accuse Jono, why couldn't the web of suspicion extend to Elan as well?

"Concentrate on the palace," Qui-Gon said. Obi-Wan heard disapproval in his voice. "I will handle Elan."

The communication faded. Obi-Wan slipped the comlink back in his pocket, disappointed in their exchange. Sometimes it felt as though he and Qui-Gon would never achieve the mind communion that is the mark of the ideal Master–Apprentice relationship.

Obviously, Qui-Gon had not been able to convince Elan that she was the heir to the crown. Why was he wasting his time with the hill people?

Obi-Wan followed the path back to the

kitchen gardens. As he rounded a corner, he almost ran into Jono.

"Obi-Wan! There you are," Jono said. "I left a tray for you. Fresh juna berries for you this morning. Very sweet."

Obi-Wan nodded and headed back toward the palace. Jono had been so close. Had he heard Obi-Wan's communication? Was Jono a spy for Giba and Beju after all?

Obi-Wan guessed that the Queen was being poisoned with her night tray, but he couldn't be absolutely sure. He had no way of knowing how long the poisonous agent took to act. He couldn't take any chances with the Queen's life.

He hurried to the Queen's chambers. The Queen sat in the outer chamber in her morning robe. Dark circles were under her eyes, and her long hair fell lankly down her back. The table was set for her breakfast — tea, fruit, and a protein cake. She was just lifting the tea to her lips with a shaking hand . . .

"No!" Obi-Wan cried. He sprang forward and knocked the cup away. It fell and smashed on the stone floor.

The Queen slowly turned to stare at it. "That was part of my betrothal gift," she said.

"I think you're being poisoned, Queen Veda," Obi-Wan blurted.

The Queen seemed to move her head with difficulty. She fixed her eyes on him. "What did you say?"

"I don't know who it is," Obi-Wan said desperately. "I have no proof — not yet. But if it is true, you must not drink or eat anything that is prepared for you."

"This is impossible," the Queen whispered.

"Impossible it is," Prince Beju announced, striding in. Giba followed on the Prince's heels. "The Jedi is lying!"

"Why would he lie, my son?" Queen Veda asked weakly.

"To discredit the palace," Prince Beju answered. "Or for some other reason we have yet to discover. I do not trust either of them, Mother!"

"And where is the other?" Giba demanded silkily. "Time and time again I have asked to see him, only to hear that he is resting, or walking about. I do not believe it! This Jedi lies already, I think. So why should he not lie about this?"

"You both are ready to accuse me. Strange that you do not give a thought to whether what I say is true," Obi-Wan pointed out. "Even if there is a chance that it's true, I would think you would be concerned. Look at the Queen. She grows weaker every day."

The Prince turned to his mother. His angry

look faltered for a moment, and he took a half step toward her. Then he collected himself and turned to Obi-Wan. "My mother's illness is not your concern. And spreading lies about it doesn't help her. It only upsets her! Perhaps Qui-Gon Jinn is mixed up in this poisoning you speak of. Giba is right. It is strange that we haven't seen him. He agreed to our rules, and then broke his promise. He is capable of anything!"

"Qui-Gon has gone to the mountains to try to convince Elan to bring the hill people to vote," Obi-Wan said. It was a half truth, but at least it gave an explanation for his disappearance. He could not reveal the Queen's secret.

"What a ridiculous story!" Prince Beju scoffed. "Why would the hill people make a difference? Why should we care what they think? Obviously, you are lying again."

The Queen pushed herself to her feet. The act seemed to cause her great effort. "He is not lying, Beju," she said. "I know it. I asked Qui-Gon to contact Elan. For me."

"But why?" Prince Beju asked, wheeling around to face his mother.

"Because she is your half sister," Queen Veda replied steadily. "It is time you knew. Your father had an early marriage, and a child. He divorced his wife and abandoned the child. The decision haunted him —"

"I don't believe it!" Prince Beju shook his head. "Now *you* are lying. Father would not act so dishonorably. Family is the cornerstone of life on Gala. How often he said that. He would not disgrace the Tallah name by marrying a hill person. And he would not abandon his child! You know this!"

"I am sorry to tell you this, Beju," Queen Veda said gently. "It is true. He regretted it. He wanted to make it right."

"You defile Father's memory," Prince Beju whispered in horror. "Will you go to any length to shame me?"

The Queen turned to Giba. "Tell him," she begged. "You were there. You know it is true."

Giba shook his head. "I'm sorry, Queen. I will do anything for Your Highness. Except lie for you."

The Queen staggered backward. Obi-Wan moved forward to support her.

"Now I see it all," Prince Beju raged. "You are in league with the Jedi. You have conspired against me. You will do whatever it takes to make sure I do not gain the crown."

"No, Beju, my son," Queen Veda said weakly. "No —"

"I am calling the guards," Prince Beju said firmly. He moved toward the tubes mounted in the wall.

Obi-Wan was still holding on to the Queen's arm. He could feel her shaking. She was close to collapse. Yet with a sudden burst of strength, she pulled away from Obi-Wan. She had time to give him a look that told him to run. Then she staggered forward and collapsed against her son.

Prince Beju was thrown off balance. He held on to his mother so that she wouldn't fall. Giba took a step forward to help him.

Obi-Wan quickly ran out the door.

Obi-Wan fled. He burst through the door to the gardens and saw the flick of a silver robe as the elder council member with the milky blue eyes moved off into the trees. Obi-Wan turned in the opposite direction and snaked through the orchard.

He had to leave the palace grounds, and he could not leave by the main gate. He was sure now that Giba was behind the Queen's poisoning. The only question was if Prince Beju knew about it. The Prince had seemed genuinely stricken by his mother's condition.

He heard running footsteps behind him. Obi-Wan quickened his pace. He was almost to the high stone wall that surrounded the palace grounds.

"Obi-Wan! Wait, friend!"

It was Jono. Obi-Wan hesitated. Could he trust him? He wanted to trust him. He liked him.

But had it just been a coincidence that Giba and Beju had burst into the room while he was talking to the Queen? Had Jono followed him there from the gardens, then run to fetch them? Qui-Gon's warning lay heavy on his heart.

"Please!" Jono called. In another moment, he would round the turn of the path. What if he was bringing the guards? Obi-Wan still had time to run.

I knew you would return. . . . I have waited for a friend for a long time, Obi-Wan.

He remembered the look in Jono's eyes that day, wistful and sincere. Jono had trusted him. Obi-Wan had to return the favor. Obi-Wan stopped short.

Jono burst into sight, his blond hair flying. He almost slammed into Obi-Wan, but instead tripped and went flying.

"Ow!" he cried, rubbing his knee. He pushed his hair out of his eyes and grinned. "That will teach me to try to catch a Jedi."

Obi-Wan helped him to his feet. "You can run fast."

"That's why you need me," Jono said. "You must let me help you. I was coming to attend the Queen. I heard what happened. Do you really think the Queen is being poisoned?" he ended on a whisper.

"Yes, I do," Obi-Wan said.

"Beju has called the guards. It's not safe here, Obi-Wan. They're already searching for you."

"I was just about to leave," Obi-Wan told him.

"But where will you go?" Jono asked, frowning.

"I'll hide in the city," Obi-Wan said. "I'll wait for Qui-Gon to return."

"They will catch you," Jono said. "There are spies everywhere. I must go with you. And I know where we should go."

"Where?" Obi-Wan asked.

"To Deca Brun," Jono said firmly. "He will help us."

Deca Brun's headquarters were in a crowded, bustling area of Galu, in the middle of shops and tall residential towers. Red banners proclaiming his name flapped from almost every window. Large posters of a smiling Deca were plastered on walls. Written on the bottom in Deca's bold handwriting was: I AM YOU! WE ARE ONE!

"It was Deca who showed us that we are all Galacians," Jono told Obi-Wan as they approached the building. "Before, family lineage was the most important tie on Gala. The great families of Gala — the Tallahs, the Gibas, the

Prammis, and others — received the favors of the court. It was Deca who said that we owed loyalty to each other, to all Galacians."

The boy's face shone with pride. "He made me realize that there was a world outside the palace." Jono pushed open the door. The office was filled with campaign workers. Some tapped on datapads, others huddled in groups, talking earnestly.

One tall, bony Galacian caught sight of Jono. He grinned and waved him over. "Jono! Come to volunteer, have you?"

Jono headed for the man. "Sila, this is my friend Obi-Wan. We need to see Deca at once."

Sila smiled. "So do we all, Jono," he said. "He's hard to track down. He's everywhere. Making speeches, meeting new supporters . . ."

"But this is important," Jono insisted.

Sila's smile faded. "I can see that," he said. "He could be in his private quarters." He hesitated. "Come with me," he said.

Obi-Wan nodded at Jono to go ahead. He took a seat against a wall. Suddenly a young woman stuck her head in the front door. "Rally on Thrush Street," she called. "Aren't you all coming? We need help."

The Brun workers sprang to their feet, grabbing banners and laser signs. "Hold down the fort," one of them yelled at Obi-Wan. He nodded.

In seconds, the room had cleared out. Someone had left a holofile open on the desk near him. Obi-Wan leaned over it.

A familiar name caught his eye. OFFWORLD.

A chill ran though Obi-Wan. He and Qui-Gon had tangled with Offworld recently. The corporation was a ruthless organization that enslaved beings for their vast mining operations. They plundered planets, depleted their natural resources, and then moved on.

And Offworld was headed by Qui-Gon's enemy, his former apprentice, Xanatos.

Obi-Wan touched the scrolling device. As far as he could make out, Offworld had donated a large sum to Deca Brun's campaign. The money had been funneled through several names of other Galacian companies.

Obi-Wan closed the file and scrolled through the remaining file titles, but there was no other mention of Offworld. Then he saw a file marked GALACIAN MINING CORP.

He accessed it. It was a detailed plan for opening up half of tiny Gala to mining operations. This would include the Galacian Sea, the largest source of fresh water for the planet — and the home of the few remaining sea people.

Obi-Wan quickly read through the plans, which included importing workers from other worlds, building spaceports for the huge transports that were part of Offworld operations, and "recruiting" native Galacians for the work.

The company was a front for Offworld.

Deca Brun must have agreed to the plans in exchange for financial support, Obi-Wan realized. Deca claimed his treasury was based on small donations from the average Galacian. It was proof of his wide support. But instead, most of his campaign had been funded by Offworld.

Obi-Wan quickly shut down the holofile. He turned and hurried through the door where Jono had disappeared. He had to find the boy, get out of there, and warn Qui-Gon . . .

Instead, he ran into four blasters pointed at his chest. Four guards stood in the hallway. Behind them was another door. Obi-Wan heard the lock click behind him on the door he'd just run through.

"Give me your weapons, spy," one of them said.

"I'm not a spy —" Obi-Wan began. Blaster fire suddenly erupted. Obi-Wan heard it whistle by his ear and thud into the wall behind him. Bits of stone flew out. One cut his cheek.

"Give me your weapons, spy," the guard repeated.

Another guard came forward. He took Obi-Wan's lightsaber and comlink.

"Do you know," the guard said conversationally, "how much food it takes to feed Deca's organization?"

Surprised by the question, Obi-Wan shook his head.

"Let me show you," the guard invited. He pushed Obi-Wan forward roughly with his blasters.

They took him to a vast kitchen area. Then they opened a thick durasteel door and shoved him inside. It was a food storage area. Boxes lined row after row of shelves, and meat hung from hooks on a far wall. It was cold.

Obi-Wan landed on the floor of the huge freezer. He heard the thick door shut, and the bolt shot home.

As soon as Qui-Gon woke, he knew the storm was over. The wind had died, and an eerie stillness lay over the camp. When he cracked open the door of the dome, he saw a white blanket of snow, and a clear blue sky.

Elan would want him to leave today. Qui-Gon gathered his things, trying to gather his thoughts as well. Was there another argument he had yet to try? He refused to give up. He sensed that Elan's participation in the election process was crucial for its success.

He ate a small breakfast and walked through the snow to Elan's dome. The hill people were already stirring. Children were playing in the snow. A man gathered late season berries from a bush. Dana waved at him from across the clearing, where he was carrying wood for an elder.

Qui-Gon knocked on the door of Elan's dome, and she called out an invitation to enter.

She was mixing salves and potions at a work table in front of a small, cheerful fire. Qui-Gon remembered Obi-Wan's suspicions. He had discounted them immediately. Had he been wrong to do so? Yet something in Elan felt pure to him, felt real. He could not imagine her capable of condemning someone to a slow death by poisoning. Qui-Gon pulled up a chair next to her.

"Don't get too comfortable," she said. "You're leaving this morning."

"The snow seems deep," Qui-Gon observed.

"We'll give you a swoop," she said. She began to rub herbs into a paste.

"My wounds still trouble me," Qui-Gon said.

"I'm making you some medicine," she answered, unperturbed. "Almost as good as bacta." She looked at him at last with a faint smile. "Do you think I will change my mind, Qui-Gon? If so, you don't know me."

"Ah," he said. "But I feel that I do."

The rumble of thunder suddenly rolled through the still air. The dome rattled with the power of it.

"Another storm," Qui-Gon said.

She grinned. "You'll make it."

The thunder rumbled again. Qui-Gon sat up straighter. When he looked at Elan, he saw that her smile had faded.

"That is not thunder," Elan said.

"Tanks," Qui-Gon replied.

When they ran from the dome, Dana was racing for them. "We're under attack," he said breathlessly. "It's the royal guard! I saw the insignia."

The rumble of tanks made the ground shake. Qui-Gon saw them approaching across a wide plain. The tanks were hampered by the deep snow, but they would make it. The hill people didn't have much time.

"We've got to divert them from the camp," Elan cried.

A shadow fell over the snow. Qui-Gon looked up. A massive royal guard transport ship banked over the camp. It landed in a snow-covered meadow near the moving tanks. Ramps slid down around the transport. More tanks rolled down.

"Proton tanks," Qui-Gon said. "The troops are inside. They won't risk exposure if they don't have to."

"The camp will be leveled," Dana said.

Elan bit her lip, thinking. "The wind came

from the northeast during the storm, right, Dana?"

"Yes, but . . ."

"Get everyone to the swoops," Elan ordered crisply. "Have Nuni take all the children and elders to the safe shelter. And send Viva to gather my medicines. We . . . we could need them later. Quickly!"

Dana nodded and ran off. Elan turned to Qui-Gon. He admired her coolness in the face of such odds.

"And you, Qui-Gon," she said. "I will need every swoop for battle. I can't loan you one now. But you can escape down the back of the mountain that way." She pointed to a narrow trail that snaked past the domes.

"I'll take that swoop you promised me," Qui-Gon answered.

"But I can't —"

He activated his lightsaber and held the glowing green light front of her. "I will not leave your people unprotected," he said.

The hill people were ready to go — everyone over the age of ten and under the age of eighty sat astride swoops, Qui-Gon guessed.

Elan swung a leg over her swoop. Qui-Gon did the same.

"Here's the plan," she told the others. "First, we buzz the tanks. Make them angry. Keep out of cannon range. Remember the zoomball game?"

Everyone nodded. She grinned at them, meeting as many eyes as she could. "Make the tanks the goalposts. Fly as though you're up against the best zoomball players in the galaxy. We're going to try to drive them away from the camp. Then when they're good and mad, we'll head to Moonstruck Pass."

"Moonstruck Pass?" Dana asked. "But —"

Elan grinned. "Exactly."

Qui-Gon didn't have time to ask what they meant. Elan gunned her engines and took off. Within seconds she was just a dot in the distance. The others followed.

Qui-Gon had driven speeders of various kinds and all sorts of flying vehicles. This was his first experience on a swoop. The engine controls, as well as the steering, were on the handlebars. He gunned the engine as Elan had, picked up speed, then corrected his direction slightly by turning the right handlebar. Immediately, the swoop flipped and headed for a tree.

"Lean away from the turn!" someone yelled to his left, and Qui-Gon leaned, holding on for dear life. Once he felt the swoop was under control again, he tried a more cautious correction.

This time he was able to stay with the others, or at least keep them in sight.

Soon, Qui-Gon had a feel for the machine. It was more responsive than he was used to, but it was agile. Before coming in range of the ion cannons, he practiced diving and soaring and sharp turns, hanging in midair and then turning. Then he picked up speed to join the others, who were almost in range of the tanks.

Elan turned as he rode up next to her. "About time," she said. Her grin was friendly, as though they were out for a pleasure ride. "Think you can handle that machine?"

"I'll do my best," Qui-Gon answered, just as cannon fire ripped into a tree to his left.

"You'll need to," Elan answered. She turned her handlebars sharply to the right, avoiding another blast from the cannon.

The swoops spread out in formation, dived, and zoomed upward again. They charged forward to the tanks, then retreated. Soon, Qui-Gon caught the rhythm. He understood why Elan had likened it to a game. The tanks were clumsy compared to the small, agile swoops. They were able to fly up high, then zoom downward into the mouths of the cannons, then turn away before the royal guard had a chance to fire.

Elan and Dana led one tank on a chase, losing it in some undergrowth. Qui-Gon heard a tremendous crash, and a cheer went up among the hill people. The tank had fallen nose-first into a ravine.

"Moonstruck Pass!" Elan called. She reversed her engines, hovering in midair as another cannon blast missed her by a hair. Then she zoomed down, heading down the mountain but constantly zigzagging from right to left, up and down. Qui-Gon followed the dizzying trail.

The tanks found it hard to keep up. Qui-Gon imagined that they had thought the battle would be simple. They would train their massive guns on the camp, destroy it, then capture the survivors. They did not expect the hill people to lead them on a chase down a mountain. If they were smart, they wouldn't follow. But the royal forces were rusty. They hadn't fought a tactical battle in generations. Most of their job had been putting down minor insurrections in the cities. They were long on strength and short on tactics.

But Qui-Gon knew better than to underestimate those tanks. Once they caught Elan and the hill people, their firepower would eventually win the day. How could bowcasters and a few blasters — and one lightsaber — hold out against such weaponry?

Qui-Gon stayed at the rear of the swoops, trying to draw ion cannon fire from the speeding tanks. He had no idea where he was heading. The mountains on either side began to close in. He began to worry. Soon, the swoops would be unable to maneuver freely, and that was their only tactical advantage.

Sunlight hit the snow ahead, blinding him. Suddenly, the swoops in front of him slowed down. Qui-Gon quickly scaled back, drifting uncomfortably close to the tank at his rear. The Force surged around him, warning him, and he swung to his left. Cannon fire missed him by inches. He felt the hot breath of it sear his back.

Qui-Gon zoomed forward to catch up to the other swoops. The sun was so bright on the snow that he could hardly see. He used the Force to guide him. He realized that the trail he was following narrowed even further, the canyon ahead curved back in on itself from above, forming a kind of bowl. They would surely be trapped there, he thought. Had Elan lost her way? Or did she have a plan in mind? He just wished he knew what it was.

He caught up to the other swoops, who were now hovering high above the pass into the canyon. Qui-Gon joined them. When the tanks arrived, the swoops would be cut to pieces.

Jedi are ready to meet death at any moment. But did Elan have to *invite* it?

The tanks roared ahead, picking up speed as the royal guard realized they were about to trap the hill people. Ion cannons boomed now, more in triumph than according to plan. The tanks rolled into the canyon. The first maneuvered to fire on the hovering swoops. . . .

And it suddenly sank into an enormous drift. Snow and ice caved in over the top. The second tank crashed through a skin of ice and was swallowed up.

It was too late for the others to retreat. One by one, they crashed through the top of the ice-crusted snow and were swallowed up as well. In just moments, the tanks had completely disappeared.

Elan zoomed up next to Qui-Gon. The cold wind had turned her cheeks pink. Her navy eyes sparkled.

"I don't think you'll be needing that lightsaber, Jedi," she said.

Elan had known that with a northeast wind, the canyon would acquire drifts hundreds of meters deep. The lack of morning sunlight would cause ice to form a crust on the top. She had gambled that the tanks would roll in, anxious to capture the hill people.

Her gamble had paid off. The hill people had won the battle without one casualty. They could have left the royal guard buried alive in the snow. Qui-Gon could not have prevented it. He could not have dug the tanks out himself. But to his surprise, Elan organized a rescue operation.

Using snow-borers that hovered only inches above the surface, the hill people dug tunnels into the snow, deep below to the tank entrances. They led the surprised and grateful battle soldiers to the surface, where they were flown back to the camp on swoops.

They were housed in the largest dome and

brought blankets. Guards were posted at the dome door, but none of the soldiers wanted to escape. They were grateful for the warm shelter. Bandages and ointments were given to those who needed them. The crash into the snow had bruised a few. One soldier had sprained his wrist. The tank that had slid over into the ravine produced one woman warrior with a bruised temple. That was the extent of the injuries.

Qui-Gon tried to raise Obi-Wan on the comlink. He needed to find out what was going on at the palace. Who had ordered the attack? Prince Beju? Qui-Gon knew one thing: Desperation had fueled the attack. That meant the situation could be volatile back at the capital.

Obi-Wan didn't answer. Qui-Gon pushed his worry away for the moment. He headed to Elan's dome.

"Now *I* have a problem," Elan grumbled when Qui-Gon entered. She was busy tending to an elder who had been grazed by a branch as he flew on his swoop. "What am I going to do with all of them? I can't set them loose in the mountains. Maybe you could lead them back."

She dabbed ointment on the elder's forehead, then gently bandaged it. "You should have gone with the rest of the elders, Domi," she scolded.

"I'm too young to be an elder," Domi said.

Elan sighed as she rinsed her hands. "Now we have to feed them all. We're going to be out of supplies in a week."

Still grumbling, Elan headed off. Domi grinned at Qui-Gon.

"She's got a soft heart, our Elan," Domi said.

"And a tough bite," Qui-Gon said.

Domi laughed. "True." He touched his bandage gingerly. "She has healing hands, like her father."

"You knew her father?" Qui-Gon asked curiously.

"Rowi's memory is still cherished by our people," Domi answered. "He knew every herb in the mountains. He passed on his potions to Elan. And her mother Tema was known for her spirit. She was one of the few to leave us. She was restless, wanted to see the world outside. But she returned. Hill people always return." Domi slid off the stool.

"Where did Tema go?" Qui-Gon asked.

"To Galu, where they all go," Domi answered. "And they all return. Tema was an artisan, and she heard the palace needed workers. She wanted to see life outside the hills. She never spoke of what she found there. I never had an inclination to go, myself. I would miss the mountains."

Smiling, Dorni headed out. Qui-Gon frowned. So Elan had lied to him. Her mother had traveled to Galu, after all. And she had worked at the palace.

Elan must be afraid, he realized. He had shattered her world, her belief in where she came from. She might push his words away. But she would not be able to forget them.

Elan had been to the kitchen dome, but had already left when he arrived. Food preparation was under control. Qui-Gon headed to the dome where the prisoners were kept, hoping to find her there.

He nodded at the posted guard and went in. The soldiers had gathered in small groups, talking quietly. Elan wasn't present. Qui-Gon saw an officer sitting alone by the heating unit. His tunic was stained, and his hand was bandaged. He stared dully at the glowing bars of the heating unit.

Qui-Gon sat next to him. "Are you all right?" he asked quietly. "Do you need a medic?"

"He said they were barbarians," the officer said numbly. "He said they killed for sport and would attack the city next. Instead, they rescued us from suffocation and starvation. He said they must be annihilated to save Galu. He said they had no mercy. Instead, they gave us blankets."

"Who said this?" Qui-Gon asked. "Prince Beju?"

"Take orders from that pup?" The officer shook his head. "It is Giba who gives us the orders. And he deceived us."

Qui-Gon had to talk to Obi-Wan. Giba had to be stopped. If he was willing to destroy the hill people to kill Elan, he was no doubt engineering some sort of takeover of the government.

Once again, Obi-Wan did not answer his call. Now Qui-Gon was truly worried. Something was wrong. His Padawan knew the importance of keeping in touch.

Suddenly, Qui-Gon felt a disturbance in the Force, a ripple of distress. It could only be from Obi-Wan. He must return to Galu immediately.

He searched for Elan, finally locating her as she was leaving the children's dome. He quickly told her that Giba had been behind the attack.

"What is it to me?" she asked, avoiding his gaze.

"This attack was planned in order to destroy you," Qui-Gon said. "If he had to destroy your people, he would do it. Doesn't that tell you how desperate he is? You will not be safe until Gala elects a governor. And that governor will no doubt be under his control, so you will not be safe even then. Giba will go to any lengths to get what he wants. We think he is poisoning Queen Veda."

Elan paled. Qui-Gon's belief in her surged again. She looked shaken. "I told you, the Queen is nothing to me," she murmured.

"I know you lied about your mother," Qui-Gon said quietly. "She worked at the palace. Can't you admit the possibility that the Queen is telling the truth? I fear she is being punished because she shared that truth with me, and with you."

Elan turned her face away. She stared at the trees.

"Gala will fall without you," he said. "I must return. Come with me. Take a stand."

Elan's eyes were stormy as she turned back to face him. "I will not be a princess," she warned.

"Nor should you be," Qui-Gon replied. "Elan is enough."

He couldn't feel his feet. Obi-Wan slipped off his boots and rubbed them to restore circulation. He had been locked inside the freezer for hours now. He had kept walking continuously in order to keep warm. He had called on the Force and visualized it as heat as well as light.

He slipped his boots back on. He reached into the inner pocket of his tunic for the river stone Qui-Gon had given him on his thirteenth birthday, when he had officially become his Padawan. The stone felt warm and he rubbed it between his palms.

He knew he was growing exhausted. He could not keep walking forever. He closed his eyes, sending a Force-amplified message to Qui-Gon. *I am in trouble, Master. Come back.*

What was Deca Brun planning? Did he realize that he was in league with a corrupt corporation that would plunder his planet? Did he know how evil Xanatos truly was?

Obi-Wan's biggest worry was that Deca would contact Xanatos and tell him he had a Jedi locked in his freezer. Once Xanatos heard Obi-Wan's name, he would know that Qui-Gon was near.

And once Xanatos knew that, he would try to trap Qui-Gon. He had sworn to destroy him.

Obi-Wan had to escape. He had to warn Qui-Gon that Xanatos was involved.

He heard faint noises outside the freezer door. Perhaps someone was coming to release him! Obi-Wan sprang to his feet. He pressed his ear against the door, ignoring its coldness.

The voices came to him dimly. He used the Force to help him screen out the other noises: the constant hum of the freezer, his own breathing. He focused on what was happening outside.

"I don't care," someone said. A boy's voice. "I've got my job, too. I've got a turbo cart full of meat here to deliver. It's already paid for. There will be no meals for a week if I don't get it in that freezer. You can answer to Deca Brun. I won't."

"No one goes in or out," the guard answered gruffly.

Obi-Wan focused the Force like a laser. *Then again, we all need to eat.*

"Then again, we all need to eat," the guard said. "Don't move, there! I'll push it inside."

Obi-Wan heard the lock fall away. He stepped away from the door. It opened, and a cart began to roll toward him, completely filling the doorway.

Obi-Wan sprang forward. He pushed against the cart with all his strength, again using the Force to help him. The heavy cart shot back, straight into the guard.

The delivery boy gave the cart an extra shove as it flew by. It slammed against the wall, pinning the guard. He let out a cry of anger and pushed against the heavy cart. It didn't move.

The delivery boy took off his long-billed cap. It was Jono.

"Nothing like teamwork," he told Obi-Wan, grinning.

"Thanks for the rescue," Obi-Wan said gratefully.

They ran down the hall and burst into a deserted office. The faint streaks of a rising sun filtered through the window. Obi-Wan hesitated.

"My lightsaber," he said. "And my comlink —"

"We can't search now," Jono interrupted. "They'll all be here soon." He tugged at Obi-Wan's elbow. "Prince Beju has jailed the Queen. She's refused all food. I'm worried, Obi-Wan. I think she's dying. Come on!"

An early-morning hush lay over the city. The gray light was tinged with pink. Galacians were beginning to stir. Cafés were beginning to open along the main boulevard as they hurried by.

"I spoke to the other Council members," Jono told Obi-Wan. "It was a risk I had to take. They want you to meet with them to discuss what to do about Giba. They've formed an alliance against him. Imprisoning the Queen was a mistake. Giba and Prince Beju have gone too far."

"First I have to see someone," Obi-Wan told Jono.

Jono shot him an incredulous look. "But there's no time to lose. Today is election day, Obi-Wan!"

"This is important, Jono," Obi-Wan said firmly. "I have to stop at the substance analyzer's. If he's identified the agent, we'll have proof that the Queen is being poisoned. We need that proof."

Jono shook his head. "We can't, Obi-Wan. The Council Ministers are waiting. I promised to bring you there immediately."

"If we know what is poisoning the Queen, there might be an antidote," Obi-Wan argued.

Jono bit his lip. "But —"

"It's this way," Obi-Wan said, pointing down a side street. He turned the corner, knowing Jono would follow.

It was only a few quick minutes to Mali Errat's lab. It was shuttered and dark, but Obi-Wan pounded on the door. Mali stuck his head out of a window on the second story. His fringe of white hair made a wispy halo around his head.

"Who is it?" he roared. "Who comes so early in the morning!"

"It's me, Mali!" Obi-Wan called. He stepped out into the street so that the technician could get a good look at him.

"Impatient young man! Where have you been?" Mali cried, pounding excitedly on the windowsill. "I have your results. I'll be right down."

Seconds later, the door opened. Mali stood in the doorway in his unisuit. A datasheet fluttered in his hand. "I am a genius!" he proclaimed.

"What did you find?" Obi-Wan demanded.

"I searched every record of chemical agents in the galaxy," Mali said. "Every engineered compound, every secret poison, every chemical . . . and do you know why I could not find your agent?"

Obi-Wan shook his head impatiently.

"Because it was a *natural* agent!" Mali roared.

"What a surprise! Who uses them anymore? No one! It is dimilatis. An herb! It grows in the sea plains of Gala. A pinch or two is harmless. But the local people know that if it's dried, and used in certain concentrations, it mimics the effect of a wasting illness. Ultimately fatal, of course."

"If it grows on the sea plains of Gala, it's probably in the palace gardens," Obi-Wan said, thinking.

"Come on, Obi-Wan, let's go," Jono urged. "We have to tell the Council."

"Is there an antidote?" Obi-Wan asked.

Mali held up a vial. "I have made one up. It will cost you —"

Obi-Wan stuffed all his credits in the elder's hands. He grabbed the vial. Urging Jono to hurry, he raced toward the palace.

Jono led Obi-Wan to a part of the palace he'd never visited, high in the tower overlooking the gardens.

"I need to get to the Queen," Obi-Wan said impatiently.

"They told me I should bring you here," Jono said nervously. "The guards are on the lookout for you. You'd never make it. They will bring you to the Queen."

Obi-Wan moved to the small window. He

looked down at the leafy top of a great lindemor tree. Below it spread the orderly rows of the kitchen gardens.

"Do you know the gardeners well, Jono?" he asked. "Are there any among them who would plot against the Queen?"

"I don't know," Jono said.

"They would have to know a great amount about herbs," Obi-Wan said thoughtfully. "Or what about that council member with the blue-white eyes? He's always in the gardens."

"Viso is the Queen's staunchest supporter," Jono said.

"A council member would have access to the Queen's chambers," Obi-Wan said thoughtfully. "But still, it would be strange if he brought food." Access was the key, he knew. The poison would have to be brought to the Queen by someone above suspicion. . . .

The thought shot through him like a laser. The green below him became a blur to his eyes. *Jono.* His friend was the only one who had access to the gardens and to the Queen. Qui-Gon had been right. Sometimes the obvious was the answer.

Jono had said he missed the sea. The poison had come from the sea plains. He had the daily duty of picking flowers for the Queen's bouquet. Easy to pick a bit of dimilatis, too. And

Jono was the one to deliver the Queen's nightly tea, as Qui-Gon had pointed out.

Obi-Wan turned. Jono backed up a step.

"What is it, Obi-Wan?" he asked. A look of concern was on his face, but Obi-Wan sensed his nervousness.

"It was you, wasn't it, Jono," Obi-Wan said gently. "You poisoned the Queen."

"Poison the Queen? I could not do such a thing!" Jono cried. "You know it could have been anybody!"

"But it wasn't," Obi-Wan said. "It was you."

Qui-Gon had often told Obi-Wan that he was often not in touch with the living Force. But now Obi-Wan could read his friend's guilt as clearly as a sensor. He saw desperation and fear in Jono's eyes. And something else: anger.

He said nothing, just kept his eyes on Jono.

Slowly, the mask of innocence dropped from Jono's face. "And why shouldn't it be me?" Jono asked softly. "Thanks to you Jedi, I was almost exiled from the palace!"

"But to kill the Queen . . ." Obi-Wan started slowly.

"Don't you understand, Obi-Wan?" Jono cried. "This is all I have! The Dunns have been part of the royal family for generations. It is what I was trained for, bred for. The honor of my family depends on me." Jono threw out his hands pleadingly.

"The *Queen* depends on you," Obi-Wan countered. "Your job is to protect her!"

Suddenly, Jono's face flushed with anger. "She would have turned me out into the streets," he said. "Once Deca Brun is elected, he will hire his people as servants. And where will I go? What will I do? Should I have to become like everyone else? Yes, I am a servant. But I live in a palace!" He flung the last word out proudly.

"Jono," Obi-Wan said sadly. "I trusted you."

The anger left Jono's face. "Then you made a mistake," he said softly. "You are my friend. I like you, Obi-Wan. But I guess I like living in a palace more."

Obi-Wan turned at the sound of footsteps. Giba was coming. He would certainly be imprisoned or killed.

"I'm sorry, Obi-Wan," Jono said. "Truly."

"Save your sorrow," Obi-Wan said, striding to the window. He leaped up onto the ledge and judged the distance to the ground. It was too far to fall. But the Force would guide him. "I don't need it," he said. Then, he leaped into midair.

CHAPTER 15

The dazzling green of the lindemor leaves rushed up at him. Obi-Wan gathered the Force from the living things around him, centered it inside himself. He flew across the distance and grabbed at a lindemor branch as he fell. His fingers closed around it, and he swung forward, using the momentum to grab at the next branch down. Then to the next, and the next, until it was an easy leap to the ground.

He didn't bother looking up. Giba was most likely already summoning the royal guards. He had to make it to the Council Chamber without being seen.

Obi-Wan slipped inside the kitchen door. He ran past the startled cooks, burst into the pantries, raced past the dining areas and found the hallway leading to the wing where the Council Ministry offices were located.

The halls were deserted. Obi-Wan raced down

the stone corridor, wishing he had his lightsaber. He heard the sound of approaching footsteps moving at double time. He ducked into the first room he saw.

He closed the door behind him and pressed himself against it. The footsteps hurried past.

He let out a breath. Safe. For the moment.

He was in some sort of royal reception room. An ornate, gilded bench stood on a platform at one end. Rows of chairs faced it. Glittering tapestries were hung on the walls. Antique weapons were displayed behind the bench.

There was another door at the far end of the room. Obi-Wan headed for it. He turned the handle and began to cautiously pull it open. Even as he did so, he felt it push from the other side. It flew open with the combined effort, and Prince Beju tumbled into the room.

He found his footing immediately and turned with flashing eyes to Obi-Wan.

"Hiding like a coward, are you? It's no use. The guards are everywhere. They can be here in an instant." Prince Beju strolled toward the series of tubes that called guards and servants. He reached toward the red tube.

"You talk of cowards," Obi-Wan said coolly, hiding the desperation he felt. If Prince Beju touched that tube, he was lost. And so was the Queen. "And yet you summon the guards."

Prince Beju hesitated. "Are you calling me a coward, Jedi?"

Obi-Wan shrugged. "I am only drawing a conclusion. Since I've arrived here, you've spoken of me as a coward. But there has always been a guard within your call. What do words mean when they are contradicted by actions? I have faced you alone, but you only face me with others who will do your fighting for you. Am *I* the coward?"

Prince Beju flushed an angry red. His hand dropped. He strode to the case displaying antique weapons. He lifted the top and drew one out.

"Do you know what this is, Obi-Wan Kenobi?" he asked, flourishing it.

"It is a sword," Obi-Wan answered. He had never used the weapon, but he had seen drawings of it at the Temple. It was like a lightsaber, only made of metal.

Prince Beju held the sword up, then slashed downward at a tapestry. The rich fabric was rent in two.

"We keep the edges honed," he said. "I studied swordfighting as part of my royal training. My father insisted." He feinted a blow at Obi-Wan, who did not move.

"Do you think you could manage one?" Beju asked. "Or does a Jedi only fight with his own weapon? That way he always has the advantage." His teeth gleamed as he smiled tauntingly at Obi-Wan.

"Why don't we find out?" Obi-Wan asked, keeping his tone neutral. He had to keep his mind focused on the battle ahead. He could not let the Prince's jibes get under his skin.

Beju took another sword from the case and tossed it at Obi-Wan. Before his fingers had closed around the hilt Beju sprang forward with a downward blow. Obi-Wan had time to twist away, but not before the sharp blade slashed his tunic. He felt blood run down his arm.

"Had enough?" Beju asked mockingly.

In answer, Obi-Wan lunged forward. The clang of metal rang through the air as Beju parried his blow. Beju pushed back against him. Obi-Wan was surprised at how strong the boy was. He was in much better shape than Obi-Wan would have guessed.

Beju pressed forward, slashing at Obi-Wan, who parried each blow. His lightsaber training helped, but he was not used to the shock that traveled up his arm each time their swords tangled. The sword was heavier than a lightsaber, and his timing and footwork were off because of it. Beju pressed his advantage, driving forward, his sword glinting as it slashed through the air. For the first time, Obi-Wan had his doubts that he could defeat the Prince at his own game.

Doubt in battle, there cannot be.

Always, in times of trouble, Yoda's teachings rose in his mind. *Belief, there must be. Belief, in the Force. Reach for it, you will.*

Yes, he had an advantage that Beju did not. Obi-Wan reached out to the Force. He felt it build within him. Doubt left him. Belief rushed in. He would win because he had to win.

The sword suddenly felt familiar in his hand. Its weight was reassuring, not strange. He leaped up on the royal bench and swooped down on Beju, the sword held high, then low, stabbing, jabbing, surprising the Prince with his moves. Beju staggered back, his sword held defensively, trying to stave off the fury of Obi-Wan's attack.

Obi-Wan's mind was clear. It was not clouded with hate or bitterness. He needed to stop Beju. He struck again, trying to loosen Beju's grip on his sword.

But the Prince rallied. Anger drove him, and anger backed by skill can be a powerful ally. Beju launched an offensive at Obi-Wan. He struck again and again as Obi-Wan repelled the attacks, feeling the power of Beju's blows move up his arm. His shoulder began to ache.

Sweat rolled down Obi-Wan's face. Beju lost

his footing and staggered. They had been fighting for some time now. Prince Beju's face was red with exertion. Obi-Wan could feel his opponent's exhaustion. He hoped it would cause Beju to make a mistake.

He launched himself at Beju again. Obi-Wan drove him toward the corner. Now Beju was at bay, unable to evade him. With a downward blow, Obi-Wan dislodged the sword from Beju's grasp. The Prince dived for it, his hands closing around the hilt as Obi-Wan leaped over a chair to prevent him.

A voice behind them cracked the silence. "Enough!"

A hooded figure moved within their vision. He wore the silver robes of a Council Minister. Obi-Wan recognized the elder whom he'd seen mysteriously appear and disappear in the gardens. "You will lose, my Prince. Anyone can see that."

"I will not lose!" the Prince howled, just as Obi-Wan's foot came down on his wrist, preventing him from grasping his sword.

"Besides, Viso," the Prince snarled, "how can you tell if I will lose? You're blind! You can't even see your own hand before you."

Obi-Wan studied the elder more closely. He realized for the first time that his milky blue eyes were sightless. With a swift movement,

Obi-Wan reached down and snatched Prince Beju's sword from the floor.

"I saw you were losing some time ago," Viso said quietly. "This battle is not the point. You have denied the truth for too long. When a man does this, he loses."

"Stop talking in riddles, old man," Prince Beju said, rolling over and rising shakily to his feet. "Your stories have always bored me."

"Queen Veda has not lied to you, my Prince," Viso replied, serene in the face of Beju's rudeness. "But your father did. Giba did. The men you worshipped lied to you. The mother who bore you did not."

"Get out!" the Prince screamed. "I will have the guards throw you in jail for your lies!"

"Then you will have to prove that I lie. Don't you want to see my proof first? Are you brave enough to face it?" Viso asked in the same calm tone.

Obi-Wan looked at Beju. He saw that the Prince could not back down. Viso had maneuvered him into a corner as surely as Obi-Wan had in battle.

"Fine, old man," the Prince sneered. "Show me what you call proof. And then I will have the great satisfaction of throwing you in the tower jail."

Viso bowed. He gestured for them to follow

him. He led them out of the chamber, through another grand meeting room. He led them into a small antechamber beyond.

The room was completely empty. The walls and floor were of pale blue stone. On the floor an intricate design of interlocking squares had been traced in silver imbedded in the stone.

"Stand in the small square in the center, please, Prince Beju," Viso said.

Prince Beju looked suddenly nervous. "The square within the square," he said. "My father spoke of this. He never explained it. He said . . . he said when I was strong enough to face what it meant, I would be ready."

"And are you strong enough?" Viso asked.

Prince Beju positioned himself in the center square. As soon as his feet hit the square, the walls began to glow. Obi-Wan watched in amazement as slender beams of golden light suddenly washed over Prince Beju in a flurry of shifting patterns. He could not identify where they came from. They seemed to arise from the air.

Then Obi-Wan noted that although the glittering beams cast shadows on the floor and walls, there was no shadow or mark on Beju.

"You see," Viso said quietly. "There is no Mark of the Crown on you, my Prince. That is for another. You are not the heir."

The Prince stepped off the square. The beams of light disappeared immediately.

Obi-Wan expected the Prince to bluster, to say it meant nothing. He expected him to rail at Viso, call the elder a fool or a liar. But the Prince did none of those things.

He slowly sank to his knees. His head dropped into his hands. Obi-Wan saw his shoulders shake.

Viso drifted closer to stand at Obi-Wan's shoulder. "Everything he knew has been taken from him," he murmured quietly. "You must help him, Obi-Wan."

Then Viso glided out, leaving Obi-Wan alone with the weeping Prince.

Help Prince Beju? Obi-Wan didn't even like him. Just moments ago, Beju would have cheerfully stabbed him through the heart.

But Viso was right. Beju had lost everything he knew, everyone he worshipped. His father was his hero. Giba had replaced him. He had nothing to believe in anymore.

Obi-Wan crouched a short distance away from Beju. "Your father acted honorably at the end of his life, Prince Beju," he said quietly. "He revealed his deception. Your mother forgave him because he regretted what he had done. Sometimes regret is all we can give to those we wound."

Beju wrapped his arms around his knees. He kept his head down.

"My Jedi training tells me that to absorb a blow is to begin to recover from it," Obi-Wan continued softly. "Now you must decide what is best for you to do. Do you want to rule Gala as Prince?"

He didn't expect the Prince to answer. But Beju raised his head. He fixed his reddened eyes on Obi-Wan. The trace of tears was still on his face.

"I don't know what I want anymore," he whispered. "I don't know anything."

"You are still Prince," Obi-Wan pointed out. "Elan does not want to rule. Until the elections, you are the Queen's rightful heir. So you have an opportunity. You can act like a Prince — you can rescue your mother and imprison Giba. If you are voted down by the people, you can leave a government that is still functioning and strong."

"Giba told me that the people would vote for me in the end," Prince Beju said numbly. "He told me that there was great affection for me. But when I walked through the city I saw the truth in my people's eyes and I could not face it. What can I do now? Today is election day."

"You can stop him," Obi-Wan said firmly. "He only wants to retain his power. He'll do it any way he can. If the people hear that the elections are not free, civil war could result. You must ensure that the elections go on."

Prince Beju frowned. "Giba is too smart to depend on me."

"What do you mean?" Obi-Wan asked.

He shrugged. "He would have a backup plan. Perhaps he has already ensured another way to win. . . ."

Obi-Wan felt discouraged. Things at the palace kept doubling back on themselves. There was intrigue piled on intrigue. He wished Qui-Gon were here.

Just then, they heard the sound of shouting in the streets outside the palace. Obi-Wan sprang up and headed for the Council Chamber. Beju followed on his heels.

They hurried to the window. Hundreds — maybe thousands — of people were heading down the hill into Galu. Some of them were on swoops. They herded a battalion of the royal guard, who marched between them.

At the head of the group rode a woman, her silver hair streaming behind her. Next to her rode Qui-Gon. Galacians were spilling out into the street to see the sight.

"Whatever plan Giba has, it's over," Obi-Wan told Beju. "The hill people are coming to vote."

Qui-Gon found Obi-Wan waiting for him at the palace gates. His heart lifted at the sight of his Padawan.

"I tried to reach you on the comlink," he told him.

"I was unavoidably detained in a freezer," Obi-Wan said with a grin. "I see you convinced Elan to come after all."

Qui-Gon nodded. "When the royal guard attacked, she knew she was needed here. Where is Giba?"

Obi-Wan led Qui-Gon back into the palace. "Prince Beju has issued an arrest order. He can't avoid the guards for long."

"Prince Beju?" Qui-Gon asked, puzzled. He hadn't expected Beju to go against his ally.

"He realized that Giba wasn't to be trusted," Obi-Wan said. He frowned. "I just hope it isn't too late for the Queen. I sent a medic with the antidote, but she's very weak."

"You've been busy, Padawan," Qui-Gon told him, giving him a nod of approval. He had wondered about Obi-Wan's ability to handle things at the palace. When he hadn't been able to contact him, he'd been worried that he'd left his young Padawan with a situation beyond his abilities. Obviously, Obi-Wan had met difficulties and obstacles, and had surpassed them.

"You were right about Jono," Obi-Wan said.

Qui-Gon put a hand on his shoulder. "I'm sorry to hear it."

They entered the Queen's reception area. Prince Beju stood waiting. "Is Elan with you?" he asked Qui-Gon.

Qui-Gon shook his head. "She has gone to see Wila Prammi. I can arrange a meeting for you, if you wish."

The Prince frowned. "I do not know yet," he said hesitantly. "First, I must set things right here. Giba is being arrested as we speak."

"I think not!" Giba said, striding into the room. He waved a durasheet containing his arrest order. "This is signed by Prince Beju. It is invalid. You do not rule Gala, Prince." Giba gave them a chilling smile. "And you never will.

When the Queen dies, another will take her place. Not you."

"I'm not dead yet." The Queen stood in the doorway. She had to brace herself against the frame, but she stayed erect, her chin high. "Guards!" she called in a weak voice to the two guards flanking her. "Arrest him."

From beneath his robes, Giba drew forth Obi-Wan's lightsaber. Qui-Gon started in surprise, but in less than a moment he activated his own.

"I do not think it wise to fight a Jedi with that weapon," he said pleasantly to Giba.

"I do not care for your opinion," Giba said, lunging toward him.

Qui-Gon's lightsaber was a blur of green as he expertly dodged Giba's clumsy blow, turned, and struck downward on Giba's wrist with a backward motion. The minister was disarmed and down before anyone could take a breath.

Qui-Gon handed Obi-Wan's lightsaber back to him. The guards moved forward to arrest Giba.

"Wait," Giba said desperately. "You do not have to recognize the Queen's order. For years, you have come to me for orders. Obviously, the royal house is out of control. Did you not see what has happened? Elan has arrived with an army! Civil war is at hand. There is only one hope. We must throw our support to Deca Brun.

It is too late for elections now. If you let me go, I will bring him here."

"And why would Deca Brun listen to you, Giba?" Prince Beju asked.

"Because I am a wise and trusted Council Minister, dedicated to my beloved Gala," Giba snapped.

"Where did you get that lightsaber, Giba?" Obi-Wan asked.

"I found it in the palace, of course," Giba replied. "You were fleeing from the guards and dropped it."

"I don't think so," Obi-Wan said. "A Jedi doesn't leave a lightsaber behind. It was taken from me by Deca Brun's men."

"I wouldn't know about that!" Giba snarled. "And I do not know what you are accusing me of."

"I am accusing you of being in league with Deca Brun," Obi-Wan answered, his tone firm. Qui-Gon looked at him, surprised. Was Obi-Wan bluffing, or did he have proof?

No one had noticed Jono slip into the room. "It is true," he spoke up quietly. "Giba was afraid that the Prince would lose the election. He went to Deca Brun with a deal. He would find him money and support from sources outside of Gala."

"Offworld," Obi-Wan said. "I saw the records in Deca's campaign office."

Qui-Gon turned to Obi-Wan, surprised again. "You *have* been busy," he murmured.

"In exchange, Deca would find a place for Giba in his new government," Jono finished. "Giba would not take the chance that he would lose his power."

"Arrest him," the Queen repeated faintly.

The guards slipped electro-cuffs on Giba's wrists, and he was led away.

"It's over," the Queen said.

Beju crossed to her. He slid an arm around her shoulders, supporting her. "Except for the voting," he said. "Let the people decide."

Wila Prammi was voted Governor of Gala by an overwhelming margin. Prince Beju dropped out of the race and threw his support to her. He got out the word about Deca Brun, revealing his alliance with Giba and Offworld. After talking with Wila, Elan supported her as well, bringing her the votes of all the hill people.

The celebration that greeted Wila's election spilled out into the streets. City people and hill people joined in cheers and song. Though Gala had been in danger of revolt, they had achieved a peaceful transition of power.

There was nothing left for the Jedi to accomplish on Gala. Qui-Gon was also concerned about the news that Xanatos had been involved in doings on the planet. His former apprentice must know by now that Obi-Wan and Qui-Gon were the Jedi who had been sent as guardians of the peace. His old enemy could come in search of him. Qui-Gon could not endanger the peace on Gala. It was better to disappear into the galaxy.

Qui-Gon went to the Queen's chambers for his last audience. He found the Queen standing at the window looking out over Galu. She wore a dark blue robe of shimmersilk. She wore no jewels, and her long hair was braided simply. The signs of illness still dimmed her beauty, but Qui-Gon saw new signs of health in the slight color of her cheeks and the clearness of her eyes.

"I have been granted something unique, Qui-Gon, and something I did not expect," she said. "I will be alive to see my legacy play out. Beju will find a better life." She gave a rueful smile. "He doesn't realize it quite yet, but I have no doubt of it. Gala will be free and at peace."

"I spoke to Elan," Qui-Gon said. "She is returning to the mountains, but she's forged a bond with Wila. I don't think she'll isolate herself so completely again."

"I, too, spoke to Elan," the Queen said. "She's a remarkable young woman. She hasn't agreed to take the name Tallah, but she's considering it. She'd add it to her parents' name, of course. Stubborn to the last."

"And Jono?" Qui-Gon asked. "Obi-Wan is concerned about him."

"Even though Jono betrayed him," the Queen said. "It is good for all of us to forgive. Jono will be punished — or at least the boy will see it as punishment. He is being sent back to his family and will learn farming. He'll be like everyone else now."

"And perhaps he will learn something about the uses of freedom," Qui-Gon observed.

"I hope so," the Queen agreed quietly. "I hope we all do." She studied Qui-Gon for a moment. "Things have ended well. You've accomplished your mission. Yet you seem sad."

"I do feel sadness," Qui-Gon admitted. "I've tried to understand why. Sometimes our own hearts can be such a mystery."

The Queen nodded. "Just ask Beju," she said. "My son is just beginning to understand himself."

"I have been thinking of what I will leave behind when I die," Qui-Gon said. "I travel from world to world. My connection to each is so fleeting. What is my legacy?"

The Queen smiled. She extended her arms to take in the city of Galu below them. Outside, Qui-Gon saw people heading to work, gathering in the squares, talking on street corners. It was a peaceful, busy scene.

"This," she said gently.

She said nothing more. But Qui-Gon understood every nuance of her meaning. For the first time since he'd landed on Gala, resolution beat again inside him, steady and strong. As a Jedi, he left behind justice and honor. It didn't matter if his footsteps would disappear, or if years from now no one on Gala remembered that two Jedi had helped to ensure a peaceful transition for their planet. They would remember peace, and that was enough.

And he had Obi-Wan. With every mission, he was more convinced that his Padawan would become extraordinary, even among the Jedi.

What he taught would live on. That was legacy enough.

And certainly, there were still more legacies to be found.

Qui-Gon had been with the Queen for some time now. Obi-Wan sat in the Council Chamber with Elan and Beju. The two did not speak to each other. Viso had asked both of them to meet him in the chamber. Obi-Wan wondered what the Council member was planning.

Viso entered the room. He threw back his hood and looked at them with his milky blue eyes, eyes that couldn't see but still knew where to look.

"Thank you for coming," he told them. "I

want to show you something. You too, Obi-Wan."

They followed him into the blue-walled antechamber. Viso directed Elan to stand in the middle of the middle square.

As soon as her feet hit the mark, the power source in the walls began to glow. Beams of light shot out. Elan's silver hair picked up the lights, making a silver-blue halo around her intent face.

The golden beams suddenly surrounded her, whirling faster and faster. Then they diffracted into an explosion of dancing light.

Elan appeared to glow. And then, Obi-Wan saw it. The outline of a crown fell on her heart.

"You see, Elan Tallah?" Viso asked. "You are Princess Elan."

Elan looked down at the shadow on her chest. She touched it, then held out a hand and observed the golden light dancing on her skin. Then she stepped off the square. The beams retracted. The walls dulled. The room became an empty room again.

"The last princess," Elan said.

Viso turned to Beju. "May I escort you back to your chamber, my Prince?"

Beju swallowed. He shook his head. "My name is Beju," he said.

Elan smiled as she held out a hand. "Come, brother. Let us walk together."

Obi-Wan watched as Elan and Beju left the chamber together, followed by Viso.

Elan and Beju had both changed their whole notions of what was left to them by their parents. They had both forged a new path, taking up a legacy based on their characters, not their positions.

That, Obi-Wan decided, was the true mark of greatness.

He, too, was on a path he had not foreseen. The Jedi Code was as much a part of him as Tallah heritage was to Elan and Beju. His ties were no less important.

He had found something unexpected on this mission, Obi-Wan realized. He had a renewed sense of purpose.

When he turned, he found Qui-Gon standing in the doorway, waiting. He wished he could tell Qui-Gon about his renewed commitment, about the questions he had struggled with while Qui-Gon was away, questions about his legacy and what that meant.

But his Master seemed so stern. Obi-Wan knew that Qui-Gon was already anxious to depart. Their next mission awaited them. Qui-Gon would tell Obi-Wan that he needed to focus on that. Ahead lay new questions, new struggles.

Always more questions than answers, there are, Yoda had said.

Qui-Gon interrupted Obi-Wan's thoughts.

"It is time to go," he said.

Obi-Wan nodded. "I am ready."

Jedi are not supposed to take sides. But on the planet Melida/Daan, young Obi-Wan Kenobi takes a side . . . against his Master, Qui-Gon Jinn.

Look for

JEDI APPRENTICE

The Defenders of the Dead

The bloody civil war on Melida/Daan had been raging for thirty years. It was a continuation of a conflict that had lasted for centuries. The two warring peoples, the Melida and the Daan, couldn't even agree on a name for their planet. The Melida called it Melida and the Daan called it Daan. In a compromise, the Galactic Senate used both names separated by a slash mark.

Every town and city on the planet was hotly contested, with territory taken and lost in a continuing series of battles. The capital city of Zehava was under siege much of the time, as the boundaries between Daan and Melida constantly shifted.

Obi-Wan knew that Jedi Master Yoda was depending on them for success in this mission. He had chosen carefully among the many Jedi Knights and their Padawans. This mission was dear to his heart. Weeks ago, one of his favorite pupils, the Jedi Knight Tahl, had come to Melida/Daan as a guardian of peace.

Tahl was renowned among the Jedi Knights for her diplomatic skills. The two sides had been close to a settlement when war broke out again. Tahl had been badly wounded and captured by the Melida. Yoda did not know if she was alive or dead.

Just days ago, Yoda had succeeded in getting a message through to his original contact, a Melida named Wehutti. Wehutti had agreed to smuggle Obi-Wan and Qui-Gon into the city and help them to work for Tahl's release.

The mission ahead was more difficult and dangerous than usual, Obi-Wan knew. This time, the Jedi had not been invited to settle a dispute. They were unwelcome. The last Jedi envoy had been captured, perhaps killed.

He glanced over at his Master. Qui-Gon's calm, steady gaze swept the landscape ahead. He betrayed no agitation or worry that Obi-Wan could see.

One of the many things Obi-Wan admired about Master Qui-Gon was his composure. He had wanted to become Qui-Gon's Padawan because Qui-Gon was well respected for his bravery, skill, and connection to the Force. Although they sometimes had their differences, Obi-Wan had a deep respect for the Jedi Master.

"Do you see that canyon?" Qui-Gon asked, leaning forward and pointing. "If you can land between the walls, we can hide the starfighter there. We can use the underbrush to cover it. It's a tight fit."

"I can do it," Obi-Wan promised. Keeping his speed steady, he dipped down lower.

"Slow down," Qui-Gon warned.

"I can make it,"Obi-Wan said, gritting his teeth. He had been one of the best pilots at the Jedi Temple. Why did Qui-Gon always have to correct him?

He zoomed into the small clearing with only a centimeter to spare. But at the last moment — too late — he saw that one of the cliffs had a small outcropping. A groaning sound filled the cockpit as the side of the ship scraped against it.

Obi-Wan set the craft down and powered down the engines. He did not want to look at Qui-Gon. But he knew that being a Jedi meant taking responsibility for every mistake. He met his Master's gaze squarely.

He was relieved to see amusement in Qui-

Gon's eyes. "At least we didn't promise to return the starfighter without a scratch," he said.

Obi-Wan grinned in relief. They had borrowed the transport from Queen Veda on the planet of Gala, where they had successfully completed their last mission.

As they climbed down from the starfighter onto the rocky terrain of Melida/Daan, Qui-Gon paused. "There is a great disturbance in the Force on this world," he murmured. "Hatred rules this place."

"Yes, I feel it," Obi-Wan said.

"We must be very careful here, Padawan. When so much volatile emotion is packed into a place, it is hard to keep your distance. Remember you are a Jedi. You are here to observe and to help where you can. Our mission is to return Tahl to the Temple."

"Yes, Master."

The underbrush was thick and leafy, and it was easy to drag large branches to cover the starfighter. It would not be visible from the air.

Shouldering their survival packs, the two Jedi headed toward the outskirts of Nede. They had been instructed to approach from the west, where Wehutti would meet them at a Melida-controlled gate.

It was a dusty hike through the hills and

canyons. At last the towers and buildings of the walled city were before them.

"What should we do?" Obi-Wan asked. "We don't want to approach unless we're sure Wehutti is there."

Qui-Gon dug in his survival pack for a pair of electrobinoculars. He trained them on a guardhouse. "I've got worse news," he said. "I see a Daan flag. That means either the whole city is now controlled by the Daan, or the entrance is."

"And Wehutti is a Melida," Obi-Wan groaned. "So there's no way in."

Qui-Gon scuttled back to remove himself from sight. He slid the electrobinoculars back into his pack. "There is always a way, Padawan," he said. "Wehutti told us to approach from the west. If we follow the perimeter, we might find an unguarded area. Perhaps he's on the lookout. Once we're away from that guard tower, we can get closer."

Keeping to the cover of the shadow of the cliffs, Obi-Wan and Qui-Gon made their painstaking way around the city's walls. When they were out of the guardhouse's sight, they moved closer. Qui-Gon's keen eyes swept every meter of the wall, searching for a break. Obi-Wan knew he was using the Force to test the way ahead, hoping to sense a break in the particle shield. Obi-Wan tried to do the same, but he could only feel glimmers of resistance.

"Wait," Qui-Gon said suddenly. He stopped and held up a hand. "Here. There's a break in the shield."

"There's another one of those black buildings," Obi-Wan pointed out. The long, low building sat next to the wall on the city side.

"I still don't know what they are, but I suggest we avoid them," Qui-Gon remarked. "We'll scale the wall near those trees."

"We'll need the Force," Obi-Wan said, eyeing the high wall.

"Yes. But a carbon rope would help, too," Qui-Gon said, smiling. He put his pack down, then leaned over to root through it. "We'll need yours, too, Padawan."

Obi-Wan stepped closer to Qui-Gon, swinging his pack off his shoulder to the ground. His boots suddenly hit something with a clang. He looked down and saw he had displaced some dirt on top of a metal plate. "Look, Master," he said. "I wonder what this —"

He didn't get a chance to finish. Energy bars suddenly rose from the ground, trapping them. Before they could move, the metal plate slid open, and they fell into an abyss below.